Jacob's Rescue

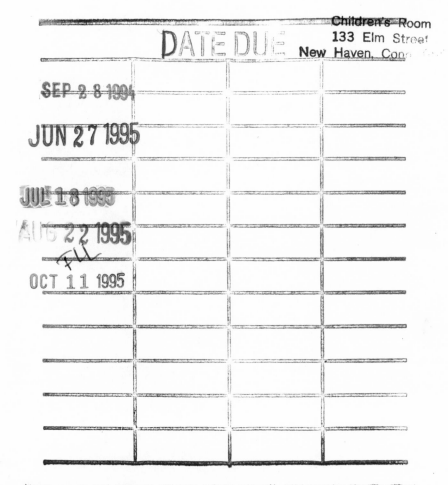

Jacob's Rescue

◆ A Holocaust Story ◆

Malka Drucker
and
Michael Halperin

BANTAM BOOKS
New York • Toronto • London • Sydney • Auckland

JACOB'S RESCUE
A Bantam Skylark Book / May 1993

Skylark Books is a registered trademark of Bantam Books,
a division of Bantam Doubleday Dell Publishing Group, Inc.
Registered in U.S. Patent and Trademark Office and elsewhere.

Library of Congress Cataloging in Publication Data

Drucker, Malka.
  Jacob's rescue : a Holocaust story / by Malka Drucker and
Michael Halperin.
    p. cm.
  Summary: In answer to his daughter's questions, a man recalls
the terrifying years of his childhood when a brave Polish couple,
Alex and Mela Roslan, hid him and other Jewish children from
the Nazis. Based on a true story.
  ISBN 0-553-08976-5
  1. Holocaust, Jewish (1939–1945)—Poland—Juvenile fiction.
2. Poland—History—Occupation, 1939–1945—Juvenile fiction.
[1. Holocaust, Jewish (1939–1945)—Poland—Fiction. 2. Jews—
Poland—Fiction. 3. World War, 1939–1945—Poland—Fiction.
4. Poland—History—Occupation, 1939–1945—Fiction.] I. Halperin,
Michael. II. Title.
PZ7.D824Jac 1993
[Fic]—dc20   92-30523
                                            CIP
                                            AC

Published simultaneously in the United States and Canada

Bantam Books are published by Bantam Books, a division of Ban-
tam Doubleday Dell Publishing Group, Inc. Its trademark, con-
sisting of the words "Bantam Books" and the portrayal of a
rooster, is registered in U.S. Patent and Trademark Office and in
other countries. Marca Registrada. Bantam Books, 1540 Broad-
way, New York, New York 10036.

PRINTED IN THE UNITED STATES OF AMERICA

BVG   0 9 8 7 6 5 4 3 2 1

J

To the memory of my aunt Eleanor, who knew how to love children.

M.D.

To my wife, Marcia, and my sons, Craig and Leon, whose love and support made the writing of this book a joy.

M.H.

Acknowledgments

This book would not exist without its heroes: Alex and Mela Roslan; their daughter, Mary Illar; and Jacob and David Gilat (Gutgeld). Our thanks to Rabbi Harold M. Schulweis who first told us about the Roslans, believing their story contained a message of moral courage for all people in all times. Thanks also to Dr. Samuel Oliner for giving us his childhood memories of wartime Poland, and to Dr. John Felstiner for his help in this project.

1

The Old Man and Woman

Marissa squirmed in her seat, her stomach crying out for food. She looked around the dinner table, which gleamed with the special china and silver used only once a year for Passover. The rich fragrances of matzo ball soup and turkey made her stomach growl, but she knew better than to complain. Her father, Jacob, was sympathetic to many things, but whenever she told him she was hungry, he answered, "May you never know the hunger I knew."

At that moment Jacob was too absorbed in leading the lengthy seder to notice Marissa's misery. Her uncle, David, playful as her father was serious, caught her eye and winked. Next to him sat her grandfather, who usually mumbled and read to himself at the seder. But tonight he stared at two strangers at the table.

Alex and Mela Roslan were not even Jewish. For the past two days they had stayed with the family, but no one said why. Marissa's father had said only, "We are honored to have them with us." When she pressed him for more information, he would only shake his head and say, "Someday you'll know why."

Although the Roslans were the same age as Marissa's grandfather, they didn't seem old. Alex joked and was hard to keep up with when he took his morning walks in the neighborhood. And Mela, plump and small, with twinkling blue eyes, stayed in the kitchen all day with Ruth, Marissa's mother. Together they prepared the special foods for the holiday.

Marissa continued to look longingly at the plate of Passover foods in front of her. A tap on the knee from Alex, sitting next to her, made her jump. "Go ahead!" he whispered, pointing to the plate. Marissa's eyes followed his finger to a hard-boiled egg.

Before she could respond, her father looked up from his book. "Alex, what are you doing?" he asked.

The old man smiled. "Jacob, did I ever let you go hungry? It's no different with your daughter."

Jacob took off his glasses and nodded, his eyes never leaving Alex. "You're right," he said softly. Turning to Marissa, whose mouth was completely full of egg, he asked, "Will you ask the Four Questions now?"

Marissa washed down the pasty yolk with a sip of wine. Clearing her throat, she sang the questions, which ask why Passover is different from all other nights.

When she finished, Marissa looked around, self-conscious because of the strangers at the table. "That was beautiful, Marissa," Mela said, dabbing her eyes with a tissue. Alex patted her on the shoulder and gently squeezed.

Marissa mumbled a thank-you and turned to her father. "I have a fifth question, Daddy," she said softly. "How do you know them?" she asked, looking at Alex and Mela.

Jacob's eyes were far away. He looked at his brother, David. As though no one else were in the room, David said, "Tell her. She's old enough."

Jacob closed the book in front of him. "Every Passover this book, the Haggadah, helps us tell the story about how our people were slaves in Egypt three thousand years ago. This year we'll tell a story not from here," he said, tapping the Haggadah, "but from here," pointing to his heart. "This is also a true story, only more recent."

Jacob inhaled deeply, and his usually calm face became tense. "When Uncle David and I were children in Poland, the German Nazis hunted the Jewish people and killed many of them."

Marissa glanced at Alex and Mela. *What do they have to do with the Nazis?* she wondered.

"Alex and Mela were heroes. They saved us," David said. Mela's eyes were moist, and Alex's hands trembled

♦ 3 ♦

slightly. The two looked so frail to Marissa. When she pictured heroes, she saw athletes or soldiers, not old people who spoke with accents.

Jacob had told Marissa stories all her life, but they were always make-believe. When she would ask him about what it was like when he was a little boy, Jacob would change the subject. Tonight would be different not only because it was Passover and not only because they had new people at the seder. Tonight Marissa finally would learn about her father's mysterious childhood.

"Begin at the beginning," David suggested. "Before we met Alex and Mela."

Jacob waved his arm at David. "How can you remember anything? You were a baby then, three years old in 1941." Then, turning to Marissa, he continued, "I was eight, the same age you are now."

"I actually met Alex before you," David retorted.

Mela raised her hands to stop the dispute. As though they were still small boys, she said, "Jacob, tell what you like, and David, you add what you remember."

"And Alex and Mela will correct us both," Jacob said, and he and David both laughed.

Marissa sat back and waited. Her hunger had disappeared. Jacob scratched at his coarse gray beard. She felt him struggling to find the words to begin his story. Marissa saw tears in his eyes.

"I remember Stasek," Jacob said after a long while.

2

Trapped in the Ghetto

He rode high in the air, on Stasek's broad shoulders. He bent his head low for his mother to pop a juicy berry in his mouth. Her laughter made him laugh, too. The sun was hot and soon they would all go for a swim. As Stasek let him down, he slipped from the man's big hands. He grabbed Stasek's shirt, but it tore. As he plunged to the ground, he heard his mother scream.

Jacob Gutgeld snapped awake, sweating. He shuddered when he remembered where he was. He heard the whispering again. A thin sheet hanging as a curtain between him and his grandmother and aunt muffled no sounds. Hide. Immediately. Trust. Money. Gestapo.

Jacob was tired, but his curiosity was too strong to let him sleep. He wished they would make up their minds and do something. Aunt Hannah told him little, but her worried face and red eyes were enough for him to know something terrible was about to happen.

Once Jacob lived in a grand house in Warsaw with his parents and many servants. Stasek, the chauffeur, drove them in their shiny new Buick to visit friends, all the while singing funny songs. Every summer he drove the Gutgeld family to their lakeside cottage, where they spent a month swimming, boating, and eating wild strawberries. When Jacob was four and a half, his mother died giving birth to his brother David. Jacob remembered little about her, only a soft blue dress and the sweet, sad song she sang the day they spent together picking berries.

The Nazis had invaded Poland and stolen Jewish homes and businesses, promising the non-Jewish Polish people that once the Jews were gone, the property would be theirs. At the same time, the Germans sent all the Poles who were strong enough into work camps to do forced labor. Jews were ordered to move into ghettos, fenced or walled areas in the city that separated Jews from the rest of the population.

Two years later, in the summer of 1941, Jacob shared one room with his aunt and his grandmother, the only ones left in his family. Other families surrounded the Gutgeld apartment in dirty, broken-down, overcrowded rooms like theirs. Day and night Jacob heard cries and shouts, but the worst sound was the rhythmic *click click* of the Nazi soldiers' boots as they passed under his window.

Because the Nazis intended to make Poland *Juden-rein*, free of Jews, every day they rounded up and arrested people at random in the ghetto. Jacob's younger brothers, five-year-old Sholom and three-year-old David, were sent away to the country. "They are too small to keep quiet like you," Aunt Hannah had explained.

Jacob's father, grandfather, and uncles had left Poland the year before. "It's not safe for Jewish men here," his father had said. Seeing the worried look in Jacob's eyes, he added, "Don't worry about these Germans, my son. They are a cultured and sophisticated people only interested in taking men to work in their factories and on their farms. No civilized country would hurt women and children."

The words were meant to be reassuring, but when Aunt Hannah kissed Jacob the night the men left, her tears wet his cheek.

Jacob didn't mind it when they first moved into the ghetto. In the beginning the Germans permitted them to have schools, shops, and other ordinary parts of everyday life. But within a year everything changed. Posters went up forbidding Jews to leave the ghetto. Curfews became more severe. Each day there was less food and there were more arrests. And the Nazis didn't exclude women and children from abuse. Jacob heard the Nazis give speeches telling the Jews that Treblinka, Auschwitz, and Maidenek were farms or factories. Plenty of food existed there. Those who were sent there would receive warm clothing. But everyone knew those places were death camps—places built to kill large numbers of people efficiently.

The only strong people Jacob saw were the armed soldiers patrolling the ghetto. He felt weak from not enough food. With everyone slowly starving in the ghetto, few tried to fight back. And the Jews knew the Polish people wouldn't help them, because they feared for their own lives.

Jacob felt trapped, and angry that his father had left him. Only those who were sick, starving, or useless to the Germans remained in the ghetto. Money helped, but no one was safe anymore, not even wealthy Jews like the Gutgelds. And besides, their resources were almost gone.

Jacob's grandmother gave him little candies from a slowly dwindling supply, but he had no patience during these hard times for her insistence on keeping Jewish laws such as not being allowed to eat certain foods. That morning he heard Aunt Hannah arguing with his grandmother. "I spent four hours finding this piece of meat," Hannah shouted, waving it in the older woman's face.

Jacob's grandmother wrinkled her nose and drew back. "I'll go to my sister's if I have to eat pork," she said, turning her face away.

Jacob's mouth watered, but his grandmother was adamant. Finally, Hannah left in anger, taking the little piece of ham with her. Jacob muttered, "I hate being Jewish."

"What, my baby?" his grandmother asked.

Jacob shook his head and scowled. "Nothing, Bubbe," he replied.

"Look," she said, holding up a dry, dark loaf, "this bread is talking to you. It has an 'S' on it. So *ess!*" She laughed at the play on the Yiddish word meaning "eat."

"No, thank you," Jacob replied coldly. *I will never be like her,* he thought as he opened *The History of the Jews,* one of the few books in his grandmother's library that wasn't a prayer book or a Bible. *If the Nazis aren't following their laws anymore, why should we?*

Now the whispering voices grew softer, and Jacob, against his will, fell asleep without a dream to haunt or comfort him. In the morning he put on the same tattered clothes he wore every day. The usual wormy black bread and pale milky tea waited for him at the table. "Eat, Jacob," Aunt Hannah called to him.

"What were you and Grandma talking about last night?" Jacob asked. He searched her eyes but found no answer. She looked away from his steady gaze. She moved the food closer to him, but he didn't touch it.

"Yankel," she said, using the name his mother had called him, "it's not safe here anymore. They're beginning to take more and more people every day." She closed her eyes. Jacob could see she was trying to erase the image from her mind. Five hundred thousand people were crammed into the ghetto. A few, like Jacob's aunt Hannah, tried to live normally. Pushcart peddlers sold pots, pans, candlesticks, and sometimes scraps of bread.

But it was impossible to deny the nightmare outside. Germans guards stopped everyone for inspection, occasionally slamming a rifle butt against a back to push someone along. Many people, suffering starvation or shocked by the sudden loss of a mother, father, brother, or sister, wandered aimlessly in the streets. Some gave up trying to live and died on the ghetto sidewalks.

Aunt Hannah tried to block Jacob's view if a cart on the street rolled by filled with bodies. If a dead child lay on the sidewalk, she took Jacob's hand and walked quickly by, all the time chattering about nothing. Jacob protected his aunt, too: he never let her know that he had seen death.

Jacob thought about all those things while nervously tearing his bread into little pieces. "Where will we go?" he asked.

"Do you remember Stasek?" Jacob nodded, happy to hear about his old friend. Putting her rough, chapped hands over his, Hannah said, "Stasek knows a Polish family, very nice people, and they want you to live with them."

Jacob pulled his hand away. "What about you and

Bubbe?" Hannah paused and looked away. Jacob knew the answer. "If you're not going, I won't go!"

"It's only for a while, Yankel," Hannah pleaded. Jacob knew she didn't believe it, but he didn't say anything more. He didn't want to make things any harder than they were. Besides, Aunt Hannah's face gave him no choice. He would miss his relatives, but he knew that going away was his only chance for survival.

3

The Disappearance of Jacob

Jacob nearly stumbled over two children crouched at the bottom of the hallway stairs. He recognized one of them, a classmate before school in the ghetto had been closed. "What are you doing, Rivka?" Jacob asked, resisting Aunt Hannah's tug on his arm.

A small, thin girl with rings under her eyes wiped her lips and looked up at him. "We spilled soup on the steps." Rivka bent her head to continue lapping up the soup. Jacob's stomach contracted as he imagined the filthy steps against his tongue.

Jacob and Hannah shivered in the chill of the late afternoon. It was almost dark by the time they reached the ghetto wall. Hannah pulled away a few stones, uncovering a small hole that opened onto a narrow alley. "Where are the guards?" asked Jacob.

"They always go across the street for coffee at four," Aunt Hannah whispered. She motioned Jacob to crawl through the hole. He hesitated. He had heard gunshots at night when others attempted escape. Now it was broad daylight. Suppose they saw him? He could be killed.

It was too late to go back. Hannah stood behind him. Ahead promised escape. They moved forward and stepped into the deserted alley. Hannah took his hand and said, "We have only ten minutes."

Jacob's stomach fluttered and his mind raced. Yesterday he thought anything would be better than being behind those high, forbidding walls, but now he wasn't sure. How could he leave his family to live with Poles? He had always been afraid of them, even Stasek, with his affectionate slaps and rough jokes. More than once Jacob had run home crying because Polish boys threw icy snowballs at him. Would this family expect him to become Christian and go to church, eat strange foods, become a snowball thrower?

"*Tante*, what's the man's name?" Jacob asked. She put her fingers to her lips in warning, and Jacob swallowed his questions. Footsteps broke the quiet as a man strode toward them. He was tall and fair, and exuded strength, nothing like the pale, sickly men left in the ghetto. He looked at Hannah and then smiled at Jacob.

Hannah leaned forward and whispered, "You are Alex Roslan?" The man nodded. "I'm Hannah Gutgeld, and this is Jacob, my nephew. Stasek said you're a good man." Alex smiled, but his eyes looked sad. "How is he?" Hannah asked quickly.

"Dead," he replied. "The Nazis caught him smuggling tobacco. They killed him."

Jacob heard the words but refused to understand them. He pictured Stasek's smiling face and his powerful hands which could fix anything. Now he was like the bodies that lay in the ghetto streets. Jacob tried to remember his dream about Stasek, but he couldn't get it to stay in his mind.

After a long pause Hannah cleared her throat and straightened her shoulders. "Stasek said you would take good care of the boy," she said, placing a hand on Jacob's head. Alex nodded.

Hannah was not reassured. "I know what happens to people after a while," she said. "They grow tired of the hiding and the running."

Alex drew close to Hannah and spoke softly but forcefully. "I don't need a lecture on how to care for children." Jacob began to feel sick.

Squatting down in front of Jacob, Alex said, "The only promise I'll make is to you, Jacob." Jacob struggled through his terror to listen to the man's words. He forced himself to look at Alex's brilliant blue eyes.

"I promise you'll be safe with me." The words felt like an embrace. "Come," Alex said softly, taking Jacob's hand. Hannah began to sob and reach for him. Jacob pulled away, angry. This was Aunt Hannah's idea. Why was she making it harder?

As he started to walk away with Alex, Jacob looked back. Hannah's face was wet with tears. Abruptly letting go of Alex, Jacob ran back, and hugged Aunt Hannah for a long time. Finally he let go. "I'll be all right, *Tante*," he said quietly. Then he turned from her and walked quickly toward Alex. He knew that if he looked back, Aunt Hannah would be gone.

Alex led Jacob down the alley and out into the street, taking long strides. Jacob had to skip and run to keep up. "From now on, I'm Uncle Alex, and you're no longer Jacob," Alex said. Jacob looked up, surprised. "Of course you'll always be who you are, but I'm giving you a new name," Alex continued. "My nephew, Genyek, lives in the country, and you look a little like him. From now on, you'll have his name. You'll be Genyek. It's a good Polish name." Alex looked down at Jacob. "Do you understand?"

He must think I'm stupid, Jacob thought, but he said, "Yes, Uncle Alex." Alex patted him on the shoulder, satisfied.

"Where are we going?" Jacob asked.

"Home."

"How long will I be staying there?"

"I don't know, Genyek," Alex said.

"What's going to happen to the rest of my family? When will I see them again?"

"I don't know the answer to those questions, either." Jacob walked silently, scowling, frustrated.

Alex stopped walking and turned to Jacob. "You're

a little old man, Genyek," he said gently. "Let me do
the worrying for a while. I'm sorry I can't answer your
questions, but I can make you two promises. One you
already know. I told you that you'll be safe.

"The other thing you should know, Genyek, is this.
You're going to stay a Jew. You'll be part of my family,
but no one will take your religion from you." Jacob still
had trouble looking at Alex, but he was beginning to
feel better. He liked Alex, who talked to him like an
adult. This man wasn't like Aunt Hannah, who wanted
to protect him but couldn't. For the first time since his
father left, Jacob felt relaxed, even when a soldier
passed, nodding at Alex.

When they finally reached Alex's house, Jacob was
out of breath and tired. He hadn't walked this far in a
long time. As they climbed the stairs to the apartment,
Jacob asked, "Do you have other children?"

Alex put the key in the door and nodded. "A boy
and a girl. Yurek is eleven and Marishka is your age,
eight."

4

Jew Boy

Alex took a key out of his pocket and paused for a moment before putting it in the lock. He asked, "Ready, Genyek?"

Jacob nodded, but he felt miserable. He remembered the big Polish bullies at school. With a wavering voice he replied, "Yes, Uncle Alex."

"Good boy!" Alex clapped Jacob heartily on the back and opened the door, gently guiding him over the threshold. "This is Aunt Mela," Alex said, pointing to the sturdy, small woman smiling at him. "And these are our children, Yurek and Marishka." *How big they are!* Jacob thought. Even Marishka was a head taller than he.

"How do you do? I'm Jacob," he said in his most

mature voice. No one replied. *How rude,* he thought, until he looked at Alex's frown.

"S-sorry," he stammered. Then, like an entertainer, he bowed deeply and said, "How do you do? I'm Gen-yek." The tension broke. Everyone broke into laughter.

Marishka came forward and handed him a small bouquet of wilted flowers. "We're happy to have you here." Jacob took the flowers and sniffed them. They were the first flowers he'd seen in two years.

"Hello," said Yurek, squeezing Jacob's hand so hard, he had to look away to hide his tears.

The small, plain apartment wasn't falling down or overcrowded as in the ghetto. It had a living room, a kitchen, and one bedroom. The parents slept in the bedroom, and the children slept in the living room. It reminded Jacob of Stasek's house. The Gutgeld family had gone from great wealth to extreme poverty within a year; this new family, the Roslans, had always lived somewhere in between.

Food on the kitchen table drew Jacob's attention. There were half a pot of coffee, a few stale rolls, and a wrinkled, bruised apple. Jacob hadn't seen so much food in a long time, and it was all he could do not to rush over and stuff his mouth. Following his eyes, Mela gestured to the table, where everyone sat down. Jacob caught Yurek staring at him. *I do not look like his cousin,* he thought, looking at the blond-haired, blue-eyed boy.

"What's it like in the ghetto?" Marishka asked.

Slowly chewing an apple slice, Jacob answered,

"Every day German soldiers come in, drag people out of their houses, and take them away on trains."

"Where do they take them?" Mela asked, her eyes troubled.

"We were told they went to work farms," Jacob answered.

Yurek broke in. "Farms? That's not so bad."

"They're being killed," Jacob replied, looking straight ahead. "They're going to Treblinka and Auschwitz."

Everyone stopped eating and became silent. Jacob's words reminded them that he was not there on a social visit. It was a matter of life and death.

Alex cleared his throat. "That's what I was trying to explain the other night when we talked about why we had to take in Jacob—I mean Genyek." Jacob looked down. He would never get used to his new name.

Yurek shook his head. "That's not what my teacher says. He says that they're sending Jews away because they caused all the trouble in Poland." Jacob stared stonily ahead.

Mela responded sharply to Yurek. "Do you think it's true? Did the Jews start the war? Did they bomb the city?"

Marishka and Yurek looked at each other, then at Jacob. "No," Marishka said quietly. "It's the Germans."

Alex looked at his watch and said to Yurek and Marishka, "It's late, past ten. You won't be able to get up for school tomorrow." Jacob winced. He had been to school only for a year before he went into the ghetto.

He yearned to return to the challenge of a teacher's questions, the smell of dusty chalk on blackboards, and the pleasure of a new book. But Alex had told him he couldn't even leave the apartment—it was too dangerous.

"I'll show you where you sleep," Yurek said gruffly, leading Jacob to a corner of the living room. Pointing to a cot, he explained, "Your head is here at the foot of the bed, and mine is at the head."

"Thanks," Jacob said, and slipped under the thin blanket as quickly as he could. Yurek got into bed a few minutes later. Despite the strangeness of being so close to a Polish boy, Jacob felt comfortable, sleepy from a full stomach, and he soon fell asleep.

When he awakened in the middle of the night, he forgot for a moment where he was. The hard cot reminded him. But he was alone. Where was Yurek? Maybe he went to the bathroom, Jacob thought. After what seemed like hours, Jacob heard a scraping sound at the window. He froze. Was it the Germans? He hid himself with the blanket and waited. The bed creaked as Yurek's large body pressed upon it.

"Where did you go?" Jacob whispered. He smelled a pungent mixture of tobacco and whisky.

"None of your business, Jew boy," Yurek snapped. Jacob didn't reply, smarting with anger and hurt from the harsh words.

In the morning Mela asked, "Did you sleep well, Jacob?" He nodded, "Yes, Aunt Mela." She looked at

Yurek and asked him the same question. He also nodded but looked away from his mother.

After breakfast Yurek took Jacob aside. He pulled out a rumpled cigarette from inside his jacket pocket and said, "Smoke, Genyek?" Jacob shook his head. "See you later, kid," Yurek called as he slung his books over his shoulder and left for school. Jacob smiled. Maybe Yurek wasn't so bad after all.

"I hate this!" Yurek exclaimed, chewing on a pencil. He sat laboring over his math homework, the subject that gave him the most trouble. Jacob was watching over Yurek's shoulder. Eight times seven equals forty-eight, Yurek wrote. Nine times four equals thirty-four. Jacob shook his head at the answers. He knew Yurek was guessing. With a little help from his aunt, Jacob had taught himself to multiply.

"Maybe I can help you?" Jacob asked cautiously. He wasn't sure if Yurek's response would be friendly or mean.

Yurek looked at him suspiciously. Then he leaned back and smiled. He pushed the paper in front of Jacob. "Give it a try if you want," he said, acting as if he didn't care.

Jacob sat down and finished the page in a few minutes. Yurek scanned the result, amazed that there was an answer to every problem. "Anytime you want to do a little math, let me know," he said as he slipped on his jacket to go out. "Hey Genyek, you're not so bad for a Jew."

5

A Nosy Neighbor

"Gin!" Jacob cried, and with a flourish slapped his card facedown. Yurek groaned and punched Jacob's arm lightly. They had been playing cards on the floor of the bedroom all Sunday afternoon. Marishka knocked but received no answer. "Yurek?" she called. Still no reply. "Can I come in?" she pleaded.

"No girls allowed," Yurek growled. Marishka kicked at the door, but the boys didn't hear because the piercing whine of a Nazi squad car suddenly filled the apartment. The sound grew louder as the car came closer.

The boys jumped up and looked out the window. Alex was running toward the building. He collapsed in the apartment moments later, breathless. When he was able to speak, he pointed at Jacob and Yurek with fury.

"You looked out the window! How stupid can you be? If I could see you from downstairs, any Nazi could, too!" Jacob felt sick.

A knock on the door stopped Alex's tirade. "Roslan, you home?" a gruff voice called.

Mela grabbed Jacob's hand and pushed him onto the bed in her bedroom. "Cover yourself with the quilt," she whispered. Putting her finger to her lips, she ordered, "Not a sound," and left him in the room.

"Roslan? What's the matter?" the voice asked loudly.

"Just a minute," Alex called as he handed Mela a sock to mend and thrust a deck of cards at Yurek, saying, "Play something with Marishka."

"She doesn't know how to play anything, Papa," Yurek whined.

"Pretend," Alex whispered as he walked to the door. "Korcek!" he said heartily. "Good to see you, neighbor. Come in."

Looking around suspiciously, Korcek asked, "What took you so long?"

"I was in the bathroom. What's your hurry? Sit down. Make yourself at home." Korcek sat down, surprised at Roslan's warmth. Usually Alex had little to say to him. "How about a vodka?" Alex offered.

Before Korcek could reply, Alex said, "Mela, bring us two glasses." He filled Korcek's to the rim.

"You're a smart man, Roslan. You always manage to have a little something extra. Like this vodka."

Alex smiled uneasily and raised his glass. "To friendship!" he hastily toasted, watching Korcek down his drink in one gulp.

Wiping his mouth with the back of his hand, Korcek narrowed his eyes and said, "Roslan, I—heard you had another kid here."

Alex's laugh sounded like a bark. "I hope not. These two are enough," he replied, pointing to Marishka and Yurek.

"I know what you mean," Korcek said, scratching his stubbly chin. "Funny how rumors start. Someone told me you were hiding a little Jew boy."

Inside the bedroom Jacob heard the man's words. He suddenly felt a burning in his stomach and an urge to vomit. Only the fear of being discovered gave him the will to swallow his fear.

Alex laughed again and reached for the vodka bottle to refill Korcek's glass. "A Jew! That's just what I need right now." He looked at Korcek closely. "Tell me, friend," he said intimately, "what would I do with a Jew?"

Korcek sipped his vodka and thought for a moment. "They're giving big rewards to anyone who turns one in these days—leather, books, money . . ."

Yurek tried to shuffle the cards, but his hands began to tremble. The cards flew all over the floor. "Ah, Yurek! You'll never be a gambler," Alex mocked.

"Not like his father, eh, Roslan?" Korcek asked, winking. He stood up. "Well, I have to go. Thank you for the drink."

After Korcek left, Mela put her hands over her eyes and let out a great sigh. Alex reached for her hand, but she pulled it away. When her husband had first talked about taking Jacob in, Mela had refused, saying, "No. We can't do it. Thousands of children are dying every day. What good would it do?"

Alex had replied, "We could save one life."

But Mela had protested. "What about our lives and our children's? The Nazis kill entire families if they're caught hiding a Jew."

Alex hadn't replied, he'd looked at his wife steadily. Finally she had said, "All right. We'll try it."

Now she said, "Alex, you know I love the boy, but I can't take this. Anyone can report us. Think of Yurek and Marishka! Is it right to do this to your own children?" Her eyes filled with tears.

Alex nodded grimly. Yurek, who had absorbed every word of the conversation, broke in, saying, "Papa, two boys in my class this week bragged about telling the Gestapo where a family was hiding a Jew. The soldiers gave the boys chocolate."

"That's why we can't tell anyone about Genyek," Alex said softly. "Now I'm going to make a hiding place for him in case this happens again. I'll be back in a few minutes."

Standing behind the door of the bedroom and listening to the Roslans, Jacob felt his mind race. *Maybe they'll want to send me back,* he thought. *I can't blame them.*

The door opened slowly. Yurek's eyes looked friendly as he came to retrieve Jacob. Without words Yurek was assuring him he was wanted, he belonged with the Roslans.

As a small boy Jacob had played hide-and-seek in the woods near his house. Once again he was hiding, but this time it wasn't a game of pleasure—it was a terrible game of survival.

Alex returned with a saw, a hammer, and nails. He examined the space under the kitchen sink that was concealed by cabinet doors. He measured the space, knocked on the walls and floor, and stood up, grinning. "It will work," he announced as he began to saw a hole in the floor directly under the sink, just large enough for Jacob to fit into. Prying the loose wood free, Alex gestured toward the dark hole and said, "Get in, Genyek. Try it out."

Jacob looked at the opening and then at Alex. "It looks too small, Uncle Alex," he said, not able to hide the fear in his voice.

Alex waved his hands to remove all doubts and tried to be reassuring. "You'll fit," he said. "I punched a few holes in the wood for air." Reluctantly Jacob dropped into the hole, stretching his legs to touch the bottom. As he crouched down, Alex slipped the floorboard over Jacob's head. The blackness surrounding Jacob made him want to leap from the hiding place, but he remained still. He took a deep breath and looked up. Pinpoints of light coming from the kitchen calmed him.

"You can't tell where you sawed it, Papa," Yurek said, proud of his father's work. Mela nodded grudgingly. Alex had indeed created an ingenious hiding place.

"Genyek, do you feel all right?" Marishka called down to the floor.

A muffled voice replied, "I feel like a mole." As everyone laughed, Alex lifted the loose board from the floor, reached for Jacob's hand, and pulled him out. Jacob's face felt hot, and his head felt as if it would explode.

"You look feverish," Mela said, putting her hand to his forehead. "How do you feel?"

Jacob tried to say "Fine," but instead he burst into tears. It was true that he felt weak and achy, but he didn't want to bother anyone. He was enough trouble for the Roslans already without getting sick.

"He hasn't eaten a thing today," Mela said.

Although there was barely enough food to go around, no matter how clever Alex was at bargaining in Warsaw, the Roslans were able to stay healthier than Jacob, who couldn't get fresh air and exercise.

Alex rocked on his heels, his hand cradling his chin while he looked at Jacob. He closed his eyes for a moment. When he opened them, he grabbed his hat and ran out the door, calling over his shoulder, "I'll be back in a few minutes." Even Jacob smiled. This was what Uncle Alex always said when he was about to embark on one of his grand schemes.

6

A White Roll

Several hours later Alex returned with an odd-looking man. The stranger's dark, pointed beard, plaid jacket, leather shorts, and hat with a large feather protruding from it were more than exotic to Marishka and Yurek. As he moved toward them, they stood close to their mother.

But Jacob shouted, "Uncle Galer!" and thrust his arms out to him.

Alex introduced the man, "This is Dr. Galer, Genyek's uncle. Stasek told me about him before . . . Anyway, I found him."

"Kowalski, call me Kowalski. The Germans think I'm Polish," said the doctor.

While Galer examined Jacob, the Roslan children stared at his clothes. Following their eyes, Alex said,

"He's a Jew from western Poland. Because he dresses and sounds like a Tyrolean, the Germans don't bother him. He's not even inside the ghetto."

When Galer finished the examination, he turned to the Roslans and said, "It's not serious, but my nephew needs to eat more, and he needs sun."

Jacob looked at his uncle as though he were as crazy as his clothes. "Uncle Galer, do you expect me to walk the streets like you? Maybe I should go to school with Marishka tomorrow. And where will I get more food? Do you think the Roslans are magicians?" Jacob was shouting now, no longer able to contain his fear and despair. Marishka and Yurek looked to their father, who seemed deep in thought.

Mela shook her head in disbelief. "I know he needs fresh fruits and vegetables, but that would be impossible. As for sunshine, what can we do?"

"Perhaps he could sit by the window," Galer replied.

Alex pulled the threadbare curtains aside and looked down into the street. "I'm afraid it's too risky. Someone might see him." Walking Galer to the door, Alex slipped some money in his hand.

"No, Roslan, no!" the doctor protested, although times were desperate for him, too. He no longer could practice medicine without being in danger of someone's finding out he was Jewish and turning him in to the Nazis.

Alex waited until Galer was almost out the door, then dropped the money into Galer's backpack. He turned and saw Jacob watching him. "Our secret, eh, Genyek?" He smiled. "Yurek, come to the basement with me for a moment."

In a while the two returned, carrying a bolt of royal blue wool left over from Alex's business before the war. Once he had sold fabric. Now he traded it for whatever his family needed.

He was about to speak when Mela said, "I know. You'll be back in a few minutes." Alex nodded with a little smile and quickly descended the apartment stairs.

Before Galer came, Jacob had been afraid he was so sick, he was going to die. He had told no one about his fear. Now he lay down and relaxed into a deep sleep.

He awakened to hear Marishka exclaim, "Papa, a white roll! I forgot what they look like." Before the war the Roslans ate these rolls every Christmas.

"I'm sorry, Marishka. The roll is not for you," her father replied. "It's for Genyek. He needs it more."

Marishka's face fell as Jacob took the roll hungrily, averting his eyes from Marishka. *She must hate me*, he thought. *I guess I don't blame her.*

Marishka leaned against Mela and sobbed. "What is wrong, child?" Alex asked.

"Nothing, Papa. I'm just tired." Marishka loved it when her father praised her for being generous. She didn't want him to know how much she wanted to rip the roll out of Genyek's hands and beat him up.

When Alex left, Marishka burst out, "Mama! Why does Genyek get everything?"

Mela hugged Marishka, rocking back and forth. "Because he has lost everything, child," she answered softly. "His house, his family, his friends. He can't leave this little apartment."

Marishka snuggled closer to her mother, and Mela asked, "Wouldn't you want to be given a little extra if that were you?" Marishka nodded, content to be in her mother's arms.

Alex had brought more than a roll. He walked into the bedroom, holding up a strange-looking contraption and said, "Look! Instant sunshine. This is a sunlamp. If Genyek can't go to the sun, the sun will come to him."

"How does it work, Uncle Alex?" Jacob asked.

"The sun gives off ultraviolet rays," Alex explained, "and they have vitamin D, the vitamin you are missing by staying inside. This lamp also has ultraviolet rays." Alex turned the lamp on, and Jacob squinted. "Genyek, cover your eyes," Alex said, handing him a handkerchief.

Jacob lay back and closed his eyes, soaking in the warmth of the lamp. "It feels like sun!" he exclaimed.

"Fifteen minutes a day and you'll be fine," Alex proclaimed. But Jacob didn't hear the instruction. He was already asleep. Alex turned the lamp to face Marishka. "Your turn, Mari," he said, patting her cheek.

7

Rat's Eyes

Jacob crouched low in the hiding place and squinted at his book. It was too dark to read, so he recited multiplication tables to himself. Then he listened to the comforting sound of Mela washing dishes overhead, knowing that as soon as Alex finished selling fabric scraps to customers who came to the apartment, he could crawl out from under the sink.

At last Jacob heard the front door close and Alex's footsteps coming toward him. Blinking from the sudden light of the lifted board, Jacob rushed to find Marishka. "Show me your homework," he demanded.

"Who's going to school, you or me?" Marishka asked, half teasing. She knew how eagerly Jacob waited for her return each day with a new lesson, but she also enjoyed school more with Jacob as her study partner.

"Let's go into the bedroom," she suggested, "where it's quiet."

A knock on the door soon interrupted them. Without a sound, Alex pointed to the kitchen. Jacob jumped up and went to the hiding place. He struggled to identify the voices he could hear through the floorboards. A child's high-pitched, lilting voice made him think about his youngest brother. *Where is David now?* Jacob wondered. *Will I ever see him again?* David, with dimples and blond ringlets, who, Jacob had been told, looked like their mother. Jacob willed his eyes open to remove the pictures in his heart and concentrate on the voices overhead.

Mela was chatting with one of her neighbors, a young woman who held her three-year-old by the hand. "Of course you can leave Gregory here while you shop, Anna," Mela said. "Don't worry about a thing." Mela led the toddler into the kitchen, saying, "Come help me cook. I'll give you some pots and pans to work with."

Squeezed between planks of wood, Jacob scraped his shoulder. A splinter pierced his skin. Before he could stop himself, a whimper escaped, but it went unheard amid the clatter of banging pots. Suddenly Jacob froze. Light flooded through the holes in the floor. Gregory had opened the doors under the sink.

Jacob could not see from his hiding place who had opened the doors. *Maybe the Gestapo has burst in,* he thought in a panic. *No,* he reasoned, *I would hear more noise. Perhaps Mela has opened the doors as a signal to come out.*

Jacob remembered Alex's stern instructions. "*Never* come out until one of us gets you. Always stay below when *anyone* other than the family is here." Jacob's curiosity suddenly got the better of him. Slowly and gently he pushed the board up just enough to peer out. He saw Gregory carefully placing the smallest pan into the largest. As Jacob lowered the board, it squeaked. Gregory looked toward the noise and caught the glint of Jacob's vanishing eyes.

"Aunt Mela! Aunt Mela!" the little boy howled. Mela ran into the room, scooping up the screaming boy in her arms. "What is it, Gregory?" she asked, stroking his head.

"I saw a big animal," he sobbed. "With black eyes! It was a giant rat!"

Mela's hand stopped in midair. *He had seen Jacob.* "No, no. no. What an imagination you have, little Gregory," she said soothingly.

"I *did* see a rat, Aunt Mela. I did," the boy insisted.

"Well, let's look around for it, then," Mela said, helping Gregory to inspect all the corners of the kitchen.

"It was under the sink." He sniffled.

Mela hesitated but walked over to the sink and bent under it. "Look!" she said with a laugh. "There's only an ugly black pot down there. That's what you must have seen. Come," she said. "Let's read a story." She drew Gregory on her lap and distracted him for the rest of the afternoon with fairy tales. To her relief Gregory said nothing more about rats.

When Anna picked up Gregory, he raced into his mother's arms, eager to leave the Roslans. "Did you have a good time?" she asked him when they reached the street. "What did you do?"

"M-Mama," Gregory stammered in his haste to get the words out. "I saw something scary under their sink. Black eyes like a big rat!"

Anna slowly turned to the boy and stopped. Looking into his eyes, she asked, "A rat? Are you sure? This isn't just a story?" While Gregory shook his head emphatically and told her in detail what he had seen, Anna thought a moment. "I have to report this," she said quietly.

"Why, Mama?"

"Never mind," she replied, her forehead wrinkled. "We could all be in trouble."

Alex walked toward them as they crossed the street to the police station. He waved and gave them a big smile. "Hi, Anna. How was your visit, Gregory?" he asked, tousling the child's red curls.

Anna didn't stop. "Sorry, Mr. Roslan. We're in a big hurry," she said, brushing by him. Gregory continued looking back at Alex's puzzled face as he and his mother nearly ran across the street.

"Times like this make me jumpy, Mela," Alex said as he sat down in the kitchen. "I look at every little thing as danger. Anna and Gregory rushed past me. She seemed, I don't know—frightened. Any other time, who would care?" He rubbed his eyes wearily. "But now . . ."

Jacob's face turned white, and he looked at Mela. "It's nothing, I'm sure," Mela said, hesitating. Then she told him what Gregory had seen. "Look, Alex," she said, touching the worry lines between his eyebrows, "he's just a baby. Anna won't listen to him."

"Don't worry, Genyek. Aunt Mela is right," said Alex. "Go find Marishka and help her with the long division homework." Jacob got up quickly, nearly knocking over the chair he'd been sitting in. "And when you're done," Alex called as he caught the falling chair, "help me with my numbers."

"I'll do it!" Jacob responded. Alex smiled.

Marishka said, "He's amazing with numbers, Papa."

Alex picked up his papers and handed them to Jacob. "Okay, give it a try." Within minutes Jacob had organized Alex's scraps of paper, some with scribbled sales and others with expenses, onto one piece of paper. Humming under his breath as he drew several vertical lines to make columns, he added the different categories of numbers. Alex, looking over Jacob's shoulder, whistled with astonishment. "I didn't realize I spent that much on muslin!"

"Here's your profit," Jacob said, circling the bottom figure. Alex whistled again and looked at Jacob, amazed at the boy's skill.

"Mari," Jacob asked, "where is your homework?"

"No homework, silly. There's no school tomorrow," she answered. Jacob was puzzled. It was only Friday, not the weekend yet.

Alex slapped his forehead and groaned. "Oh, no. It's Good Friday. That means Easter. And that means Vladek is coming."

Mela responded, "So?"

"So it means I'll have to hide what little vodka I have from your brother," Alex told her. Yurek and Marishka giggled. Uncle Vladek sometimes was a little bit drunk, but he was always a lot of fun.

Easter. Jacob knew only a little about it. Polish people went to church, and afterward children went on egg hunts. Since he didn't get to go anywhere, Jacob didn't have to worry about following an unfamiliar ritual. But Vladek sounded a little like Stasek, and Jacob looked forward to meeting him.

On the morning of Easter Sunday Jacob stayed by himself in the apartment for the first time. Silence surrounded him, making him sharply aware of how he never had a moment alone. Before the war he loved to play and read for hours in his room. But now he didn't like the feeling. He felt safe with Alex and Mela. Yurek and Marishka often took away his homesickness.

He jumped at the familiar squeal of the front door. He ran to greet the Roslans and Vladek, despite feeling shy in Yurek's hand-me-downs while the family were dressed in their finest clothes. Vladek, a large man with

a bright red nose, stepped forward and shook Jacob's hand warmly. When the children had left the room, Vladek swigged vodka and said to Alex, "Maybe that's why you always get what you want."

"What do you mean?"

"You take chances, like hiding that little Jew boy. Me, I'm afraid, but not you. And," he went on, wagging his finger at Alex, "you like fooling the Nazis."

Alex shook his head. "Vladek, I don't enjoy risking my life."

"Then why—" A harsh pounding interrupted Vladek. Alex ran to the bedroom and grabbed Jacob to get him to the hiding place. Yurek and Marishka entered the living room just as the door burst open with the force of three Polish policemen.

"How dare you?" Alex bellowed. "What right do you have to break into my home?"

The leader of the trio flashed his badge. He was a lieutenant with the Polish police. "Where is the Jew?" he demanded.

Vladek stared at the middle man. Swaying slightly, he burst out, "Jaworski! Remember me? From the Three Roses bar?"

The man cocked his head, considering Vladek. Then his face lit up. "Vladek! Sure! Good man! Say," he said, remembering his purpose, "what are you doing here?"

"I'm here with my sister and brother-in-law. What

are *you* doing here? is the question. These are good Poles. They don't break laws. How about a drink?"

Jaworski reluctantly shook his head. "No, no, I'm working. We got a report there was a Jew here and—"

Vladek cut him off with a snort. Slapping his friend on the shoulder and looking him squarely in the eye, he asked, "Do you think I'd stay in a house with a Jew?"

Jaworski reflected a moment, then shrugged his shoulders. "You don't know how many calls we get every day. People want rewards." He looked at his hands. "Mind if I wash up? I've been poking around basements all day."

Mela nodded and turned on the faucet in the kitchen. When Jaworski finished rinsing his hands, he reached down for a towel, but before he could open the cabinet, Yurek handed him one. The policeman patted him on the head and told him, "You're a good boy. Anytime you want to help us find Jews, let me know."

Yurek saluted and enthusiastically replied, "Yes, sir!" He closed the door behind Jaworski, and tapped on the floor over Jacob's head to let him know he could come out. Jacob popped up in time to see Yurek hold his nose and stick out his tongue. The boys shook hands. They both had sweaty palms.

8

The Mouse in the Couch

Jacob opened his small, worn suitcase and neatly placed within it his few clothes, a pencil, a scrap of paper, and two books Marishka had given him. Its musty smell reminded him of Aunt Hannah. Yurek's grunts and groans as he and Vladek strained to close a bulging trunk brought Jacob back to the present. Except for the opening and closing of drawers, and an occasional murmured instruction, the house was quiet.

The police visit had been a close call. Alex had immediately gone out to look for another apartment, and they were moving that morning.

"Galer!" Mela exclaimed, greeting Jacob's uncle warmly. "Yes, yes, go in to see Genyek. But remember," she said, gesturing to the boxes surrounding them, "we're in a hurry."

Walking into the bedroom, Galer gently pinched Jacob on the cheek. "You look much better." Jacob didn't lift his head. Dr. Galer raised Jacob's chin to find his eyes brimming with tears. "I heard what happened," he said softly.

Jacob swallowed, unable to speak. Alex and Mela had told him a dozen times it wasn't his fault. "This is a terrible time. Everything is crazy," Alex had said. And Mela had added, "How could you know Gregory would see you?" Still, Jacob blamed himself.

Galer had no words to console his nephew. Instead he told him, "I saw Sholom a few days ago." Jacob brightened at the mention of his brother's name. Galer didn't tell him how thin, dirty, and sickly the boy appeared. "He is safe in a house in the country."

"And little David is on a farm." Galer chuckled. "He's so smart. He makes believe he's very shy and doesn't want the farmer's wife to help bathe or dress him. Really, he wants to hide his circumcision from them." His voice dropped. "I don't know how long I can keep the boys where they are." Every bit of money Galer could get went to pay the Poles to hide Sholom and David.

Jacob nodded soberly. He felt lucky to be with the Roslans. Despite the hiding, the lies, the plans, and the everyday struggle just to stay alive, life was normal in this generous and loving family. Once in a while, in the midst of a card game or a math problem, Jacob even forgot the past and didn't worry about the future.

Galer stood and stretched his tall, increasingly gaunt frame, then bent to pick up Jacob's featherweight suitcase to carry into the living room. Alex took Galer aside and whispered, "The new place we're moving to is not in as nice a neighborhood, but it's bigger." After a quick look to be sure Mela couldn't hear, he added, "We could take another boy."

Galer grabbed Alex's hands. "Thank you, Roslan. The middle boy, Sholom, should be moved. He's living in—" His voice caught. "In a goat shed. He shares a bed—and food scraps—with a goat." Reaching into his pocket, Alex handed some money to Galer, who began to protest but abruptly stopped. Who was he kidding? He had no savings left; every day grew harder. "Thanks, Roslan. After the war . . ."

Alex silenced him with a wave of the hand. "We'll worry about that later. Now let's take care of the boys."

While they spoke, Vladek watched them carefully, frustrated at not being able to hear the conversation. Turning to Mela, he asked, "Why does your husband have to be a hero? How long will you keep this Jew boy?"

Every night Mela lay awake with fear, worrying constantly whether they were doing the right thing. How many more times would they have to move? Would they make one fatal mistake? Yet she would never send Genyek away. She replied, "And what will happen to the boy, Vladek? He'll be killed."

Vladek shrugged. "Mela, enough is enough. You

have children of your own." He paused, placing a hand on his chest. "What about them?"

"Look, Vladek," Mela said slowly, as though she were speaking to a very young child. She loved her brother, but she knew he would never understand. "You don't want to stay with us. Go where you won't have to worry about your own neck." She spat out the last word, causing Vladek to wince.

Vladek smiled pathetically. "I always knew Alex was crazy. You've been married to him so long, you're crazy, too." Then he took Mela's hand. "And I must be crazy, too, because I want to stay and help."

"Good, then. Let's help Alex with the couch," she said, taking a last look at their home.

Alex stood by the sofa. Lifting up a cushion, he said, "Climb in, Genyek."

Jacob shuddered, looking at the hole Alex had cut under the cushion. "I won't be able to breathe."

"You still don't trust me?" Alex asked in mock exasperation. "I drilled holes underneath for you. Besides, do you have a better disguise for walking the streets of Warsaw with your curly black hair and brown eyes?"

Jacob shook his head, angry and ashamed and confused.

"Climb inside, then," Alex said gently.

Jacob disappeared into the couch through the hole cut under the cushion. Almost immediately he popped his head up. "Uncle Alex, it's hot and dark!"

"Make believe you're a mouse," Marishka said. Jacob

giggled and squeaked his answer, dropping down once more.

As if by magic, the couch rose into the air as Alex, Yurek, and Vladek lifted it onto a cart. Jacob felt the thud of boxes being piled on top of the couch. *Good luck to the Germans if they can find me under all this,* Jacob thought with grim satisfaction.

The warmth and softness within the sofa, along with the cart's wheels rhythmically bumping over the cobblestone street, lulled Jacob like a baby in a cradle until a sharp German command jerked him into alertness. On the way to the new house they were passing Nazi soldiers.

An image of Alex smiling and waving to everyone, calm, confident, and privately thrilled to be fooling the Germans, helped Jacob relax back to sleep.

> *The top of the Buick convertible was down. He loved the wind in his hair. As they drove to the country, he said, "Mama, Don't wear that babushka on your head! The air feels wonderful! And I can't see your face." His mother laughed as he untied the babushka. Still he could not see her face.*

The cart abruptly stopped. Jacob found himself floating once again through the air. *We must be at the new apartment,* he thought. *At least we'd better be there,* he worried a moment later, fighting a powerful urge to peek ever so slightly out of the couch. A moment later

the couch touched the ground. Yurek threw off its cushions and said, "Okay, mouse, crawl out."

Still cautious, Jacob slowly poked his head up, finding himself in a large, empty room. "Our new home?"
he asked as he struggled to free himself from the couch.

"Yes," Alex answered. "Look around, but remember—"

"I know, don't go near the windows. Right?"

Alex shook his finger at him, smiling. He wanted
this especially bright little boy to survive.

As the children wandered through the four rooms,
marveling at the extra space, Vladek moved toward
Mela, who was busy unpacking boxes, and asked, "How
long do you think you can keep him a secret?"

Mela stood up and faced her brother, wondering what
to do about his fear. How trustworthy was he?

"It's not a problem anymore," Alex said, stepping
between Mela and Vladek. "At least not for you. Go
home, Vladek. Now. And keep your mouth shut."

Before Vladek could say a word, Mela said, "Don't
worry about us. It's only when you're unsure that you
make mistakes." Looking from Alex to Mela, Vladek
found no uncertainty. They were kicking him out.

Picking up his knapsack, he waved good-bye to Alex,
Mela, and the children.

"Good luck," he said softly, closing the door. He
took a swig from his flask to celebrate his relief at being
out of danger.

9

Sholom

The only sounds at dinner were those of knives and forks clinking against plates. Mela and Alex had argued loudly enough for Jacob, Yurek, and Marishka to know precisely why the Roslans weren't talking to each other throughout the meal. When Alex needed salt, he growled at Marishka, "Tell your mother to pass the salt." Mela shoved the shaker down the table and resumed eating.

The children ate quickly and asked to be excused from the table. As soon as they left, Alex leaned forward toward Mela and pleaded, "Mela, please, please, think about this again."

"No, Alex, a thousand times, no! You're not going to have your way this time." She folded her arms across her chest.

"Mela, the boy is hiding in a filthy space no bigger than this," he said, showing her with his hands.

"It's hard enough with one Jewish child!"

"If they catch us with one, we might as well have two," Alex said, shrugging his shoulders.

Mela burst into tears. "You think this is a joke? It's not funny!"

He nodded sadly and took her in his arms. "I'm afraid, too," he murmured. "But if we don't take Sholom, what's going to happen to him? The people hiding him are too frightened. If someone doesn't do something, he'll end up in a camp."

Mela shook her head slowly. "What kind of world is this that hurts children? To save a child we risk our own!" she said with anguish in her voice. "How can I make such a choice? What can I say?" she whispered, closing her eyes, her shoulders drooping.

The move to the new apartment, the daily struggle to feed the children and keep them healthy, the strain of constantly being on the lookout for informers, and now playing God with a child's life had taken all her strength. "Maybe Vladek is right. We are crazy," she said with a sigh. "Tell Galer to bring the boy."

Several days later, just after dawn, a soft knock on the door awakened the household. Yurek pointed to the closet, and Jacob leaped in. Alex opened the door to find Dr. Galer holding the hand of a boy whose face was so thin, his eyes were all Alex saw. He was five but looked three. "Roslan," Galer said, "this is Sholom."

Mela and Marishka entered the room, with Marishka clinging to her mother. She had never seen such an emaciated child.

When Alex challenged Mela with questions such as "What good is your God who allows children to suffer? What kind of God teaches our children lessons about cruelty?" she refused to reply. Now she muttered under her breath, "God in heaven, do you see this?"

Stepping forward slowly, Mela smiled and knelt down to the boy. Immediately Sholom dodged behind his uncle. "Hide me!" he cried.

"You don't have to be afraid," Mela said sadly. It would take time to gain this frail, terrified child's trust.

"Genyek!" Alex called. Jacob poked his head through the door. At the sight of Sholom he rushed in. Even though his brother smelled slightly of goat, Jacob hugged him tight. Sholom had once been chubby, but now Jacob could feel his ribs through his coat. Jacob scratched Sholom's scalp the way he used to like it, but Sholom couldn't feel his fingers, because his hair was matted and buried under dirt.

Jacob suddenly remembered how their nanny would scold them for playing in the mud. Constantly warning the children against filth and germs, she made the boys endure frequent baths and shampoos. Every day they put on freshly ironed clothes. What would their nanny do now if she could see Sholom?

"I want to go home, Jacob," Sholom said, whimpering. "Take me home."

Jacob hugged him. "We'll go home soon. But this is a nice place. No one is going to make you sleep with animals here."

Marishka had left the room for a minute. Now she returned with one hand behind her back. "You can sleep with this if you want." She handed Sholom a worn teddy bear. The child, however, continued to cling to his brother.

Mela put a sandwich on the table and signaled to the family to leave the room. Only the brothers remained. Jacob asked Sholom, "Want to eat?"

Sholom nodded with his thumb in his mouth. "Wait," he said, stopping to pick up the bear and bring it to the table. Sholom brought the tattered toy to his face and rubbed its scraggly fur against his upper lip. As Sholom picked at the sandwich, Jacob felt an impulse to hug him again, keep him close, the way his brother held the little bear.

Mela and Alex peeked behind the door, watching the scene. "Two is the same as one," Mela whispered, squeezing Alex's arm. "Let's call him Orish, Little Alex. Isn't that what they called you as a boy?" Alex nodded, smiling.

10

Scarlet Fever

"Papa, I feel sick," Yurek whispered to his sleeping father. Alex's eyes snapped open. In the darkness he saw his son leaning over him, clutching his head. Alex jumped out of bed and took Yurek into the kitchen. Alex put on the light and put his hand to the boy's burning, flushed cheeks. He had a high fever.

When Jacob first left the rat-infested ghetto, Warsaw seemed clean to him. These days, in 1942, he saw sick people everywhere. Mela boiled the family's drinking water, because German bombings had contaminated the wells. Uncle Galer told Jacob the hospitals were full and the doctors had no medicine to give patients. Despite this, they had remained healthy. Now, with one of them sick, none of them might be strong enough to withstand infection.

The next morning Galer examined Yurek. Alex and Mela hovered nearby. "Scarlet fever," announced Galer. "Let me check the others. It's very contagious." He took each child's temperature, listened to their heartbeats, and felt for swollen glands.

When he finished, Galer took Alex and Mela into the living room and said, "Only Genyek doesn't have it. Yurek must get to a hospital immediately. Marishka is strong, and her case is not too bad. As for Orish, his case is mild, but he's so weak." Galer scratched his beard. "I don't know what to say. We can't take the chance of sending him out. If they discovered he's Jewish, it would be the end of him and your family. We'll have to treat him here."

When Alex took Yurek to the hospital, Jacob and Sholom moved into the same room. "Jacob?" Sholom asked in a small voice.

"My name is Genyek, Orish," Jacob responded irritably from his book.

"Am I going to die . . . Genyek?" Sholom asked.

Looking at Sholom's white face, Jacob felt guilty for his impatience. "You're not going to die," he answered, forcing a smile on his face. "We're invincible, remember? Nothing can happen to us." Sholom's face relaxed, and he let out a deep breath. Surely his brother wouldn't lie to him. For Jacob it was unthinkable that Sholom wouldn't get better. He quickly hushed the nagging voice reminding him that many unimaginable things had happened already.

"Boys," Mela called to them from the doorway, "I'm going to visit Yurek at the hospital. Be sure to drink all the water I left on the night table. If you need something, call Marishka."

Mela stepped into the dim hospital ward. Every bed was filled. Some patients lay on mattresses on the floor. Groans echoed through the room. Casting her eyes anxiously about for her son, she saw his waving hand. "Mama!" he called.

"Oh, Yurek, you look so much better," Mela said, kissing him as she sat down on the edge of the bed. "How about some home-cooked food?" she asked, pulling out a potato dumpling for him. He eagerly reached for it and took a big bite. "Now I know you're better." Mela smiled.

When he was finished, he drew his mother close to him and whispered, "Look," pointing under his pillow at several envelopes containing pills. "I've been saving half my medicine for Orish," Yurek said. "And I wrote down all the directions for you."

"I'm proud of you," she whispered, quickly putting the medicine in her bag. She looked at Yurek, already a head taller than she and showing traces of a mustache. The war had turned him into a man too soon, but at least he was a good man.

Mela ran into Galer as she arrived home. After inquiring about Yurek, he told her, "I just examined the children. Marishka and Genyek seem fine, but Orish has some kidney problems. If he gets past it, he'll start to get better quickly."

Mela didn't want to ask what would happen if he didn't "get past it." Instead she showed him the medicine Yurek had given her.

"Wonderful," Galer exclaimed. "I can't get my hands on this anymore. It could make a real difference with Orish," he said as he exited the apartment.

Mela coaxed the medicine into Sholom with a little sugar water. "Maybe it's my imagination," she told him, "but both my boys look better today." Hoping she was right, Sholom smiled weakly as she bathed him with a cold cloth to bring down his fever.

That night Sholom's moans disturbed Jacob's sleep. "Are you awake?" he asked. There was no reply.

"I don't feel so good," Sholom finally answered. His hair was damp, and perspiration made his clothing cling to his body. "Maybe if I go to the bathroom, I'll feel better." Hearing their voices, Alex and Mela entered the room. Sholom tried to smile.

"I'll take you to the toilet," Alex said, carrying the boy in his arms. Jacob followed, holding his brother's hand. Mela put a cool, wet cloth on the little boy's head.

"Feel better?" Alex asked. Sholom smiled into Alex's eyes. He put his head on Alex's shoulder and closed his eyes.

Jacob felt Sholom's hand loosen its grip. To his question, "Is he sleeping?" he got no reply. Instead, Mela took his hand from Sholom's and held it tightly. Sobs racked Alex's shoulders. Gently he laid Sholom on the bed and closed his eyes.

"He's dead?" Jacob asked.

Nodding once, Mela put her hands on his shoulders. "He didn't suffer, Genyek."

"That's good," Jacob said automatically. As Mela reached out to him, he pulled away. If he allowed the embrace, he might cry, not only for Sholom but for everyone and everything he'd lost. He sniffed back a few tears, pushing down the grief rising inside him. When he thought about his parents or the time in the ghetto, it seemed as if it were something that had happened to some other boy, as though it were only a story or a movie he had once watched. Maybe one day he would feel the same about this night.

He turned to Alex and asked, "What will you do with him?"

Alex looked down. "I don't know, Genyek." He sighed. "But we have to do it right. We have to bury him the proper way."

Alex searched for the largest wicker trunk he could find, but it was only four feet long. He would have to bury Sholom sitting up. As he dug a hole in the basement, he recalled a story that Zenek, a young cripple who worked in the cemetery, had once told him. "Jews are buried sitting up," Zenek said, repeating the tall tale, "because when the Messiah comes, they want to be able to spring out of the grave to greet him."

Alex whispered to Sholom, "Little one, you'll be the first to see the Messiah."

He gently closed the lid, covering it with earth.

11

Yurek's Secret

Yurek waited impatiently for the trucks filled with armed Germans to pass. Only a couple of years older than he, the soldiers waved to him, but he only glared back. He and Jacob spent many nights talking about how much they hated the Nazis and what they would do if they caught one.

Suddenly a man grabbed Yurek by the collar, clamped a hand over his mouth, and threw him into a doorway.

As Yurek kicked and clawed to get free, a deafening explosion knocked both of them over. Blinking his eyes against the blinding light to see what happened, Yurek flinched at flames erupting from the street while cars and trucks bounced like toys. Bloody, screaming soldiers flew in all directions. The few who tried to walk were shot down by gunfire from surrounding buildings.

Within minutes everything was still. Only smoke, flame, and bodies remained. Trembling, Yurek found himself free. The man who tackled him stood quietly at his side. Yurek liked the look of his attacker. His bushy eyebrows and drooping mustache made him look both fierce and brave.

"Tell everyone you meet—Poland still lives." Even though the man wasn't in uniform, Yurek wanted to salute him. But he had already vanished between the buildings just as mysteriously as he had appeared moments before.

Yurek broke into a run to catch him. "Listen," he huffed, "I want to help."

The man turned and examined Yurek. All at once Yurek felt too small, too weak. After a moment the man said, "All right. Meet me here at midnight."

"Tonight?" Yurek asked nervously. "What about the curfew?"

The man chuckled. "If you're worried about the curfew, then forget it, boy," he said, and turned on his heel to leave.

"No!" Yurek called. "I'm not a boy. I'm almost fifteen." He had just celebrated his thirteenth birthday in January. "I'll be here, don't worry. At midnight."

The man laughed icily and said, "We'll see." Then he disappeared in the winter darkness of the late afternoon.

Yurek twitched and shifted in bed, glancing at his watch every ten minutes. It was only nine P.M. How would he stay awake until midnight? Jacob turned and looked at him. "You can't sleep, too?" Yurek snorted irritably, not wanting to explain anything, and tried to remain still.

He wore his clothes to bed, which wasn't unusual when the weather was as cold as it was that night. He peered at his watch again, it was five minutes to twelve. He must have fallen asleep! He picked up his shoes and was about to slip out through the kitchen when Jacob asked sleepily, "Where are you going?"

Since Sholom had died, Yurek rarely went out at night. Whether it was to keep Jacob company or because the streets were more dangerous, Jacob didn't know, but he was grateful. Even though Sholom had been with them for only a few months, his death made Jacob feel more alone than ever before.

"Have a drink and smoke for me," he said forlornly.

Yurek stopped. "No, no, Genyek, this isn't fun and games. I'm going to work with the Resistance, the Partisans," he whispered proudly.

Jacob's eyes widened. "Oh, Yurek, I wish I could go with you!"

Yurek playfully punched his shoulder. "I'll kill a German for you, kid," he said. "I'll be back before morning. And don't tell anyone," he warned.

Jacob didn't sleep the rest of the night, anxiously waiting for Yurek. By the time Mela called the family to their meager breakfast of weak tea and stale bread, he still had not returned.

"Where's Yurek?" Alex asked immediately. Everyone turned to Jacob. He was about to say he hadn't known Yurek was gone until he woke up, but Alex's face told him the lie would never work.

"He had something important to do last night," he stammered.

"What time did he leave?" Alex demanded, slamming his hand on the kitchen table. "What time did he leave? It must have been after curfew. The Germans shoot anyone on sight." Mela shivered and drew her sweater around her.

Marishka narrowed her eyes. "I bet he went out drinking again."

Jacob looked at Alex, who shook with fury and terror. While he prayed for Yurek to walk in and save him, divine inspiration, with Marishka's help, came to his aid. Pulling a shamefaced expression, he said, "Well, I didn't want to tell, but . . . yeah, he sneaked out for a smoke and a vodka with Jan last night."

Color returned to Alex's face. Jan lived in the same building. That meant Yurek had never been on the street. Afraid to look Alex in the face, Jacob prayed Alex and Mela believed him. Then he heard the door open and close. Mela called anxiously, "Yurek?"

Yurek walked slowly into the kitchen. His parents' faces were more frightening than anything he'd encountered during the night. What did they know?

He looked at Jacob, who flashed him a lightning-quick wink. "I'm sorry, Yurek," Jacob blurted, "I had to tell them you went drinking last night—"

Alex shouted, "You're a bum like your uncle Vladek! How dare you go out drinking at your age? Some example you make for Genyek and Marishka!"

Fighting back a relieved laugh, Yurek looked down. "I'm sorry, Papa," he mumbled. "I promise. I won't do it again."

Mela looked at Alex, their eyes coming to silent agreement. Putting her arm across the boy's shoulders, she said to him, "Breakfast is on the table."

12

The Operation

An ugly, green-clad, jackbooted Nazi forced a gun into Jacob's right ear. As he struggled to free himself, his ear exploded.

Crying out, Jacob found not a Nazi beside him but Yurek. Jacob clutched his ear and whimpered. "Get up," Yurek directed, and led him to his parents' bedroom.

Alex switched on the light in the bedroom. Jacob's flushed face confirmed his fears. "Scarlet fever," he said.

"That's what killed my brother." Jacob sobbed.

Mela drew him to her. "You're strong, Genyek, very strong. Tomorrow we'll get your uncle, Dr. Galer, here," she told him.

Jacob felt a little better, but still he cried, "I don't want to die, Uncle Alex."

Alex looked him in the eye the same way he had when they first met. "You won't die, Genyek." Then gently he said, "Go to bed."

Jacob had made Sholom the same promise. But this was a promise from Alex. Alex never gave up. He always had a plan.

Galer took the stethoscope from his ears. Alex and Mela gripped each other's hands. "The boy has scarlet fever, and it's infected the mastoid, the bone behind his ear. We have to scrape the bone and drain the infection if he is to be saved. I can't operate here. I don't have the instruments or medicine. He has to go to the hospital."

"But that's impossible," Alex exclaimed. Galer was writing something on a pad.

"Go to this doctor. I've written down the problem." In response to Alex's frown Galer added, "He's a good man. He won't turn away a child."

"Get dressed, Genyek," Alex ordered. "We're going to the doctor." Within minutes Jacob was ready. All of a sudden the pain seared through his head like a hot needle. He curled up in a ball, holding his buzzing ear. He never imagined anything could hurt this much.

"Sit up," Galer said, "while I wrap this bandage around your face." Jacob was about to say the bandage wouldn't help his pain, but then he realized it was a disguise, another way to hide. *Oh, well,* he thought, *better to look like the Frankenstein monster than a squashed mole or mouse.*

No one gave Jacob a second glance as they took the bus to Dr. Masurik's office; wounded and sick people were no novelty in Warsaw. They entered the doctor's office through a back door. Masurik came out within minutes, examined Jacob's ear, and exclaimed, "He'll have to be treated right away."

Alex said, "But he's . . . I mean, how can you . . . ?"

Indignantly Masurik brushed off his objection. "I don't care what the child is. He's sick and needs treatment or else he'll die."

"What do I have to do?"

"Get him to the hospital," the doctor replied. "Only one problem. I need money to bribe my operating nurse. Unless she's paid, she might report all of us to the authorities."

"How much do you need?" Alex asked. When Masurik told him at least ten thousand zlotys, Jacob lay back down, defeated. That was as much money as Alex made in a year! There was no way anyone, even Alex, could get that much money immediately. The Roslans had nothing to sell anymore. But as Alex rewound the bandage on Jacob's head, he didn't seem concerned. He was thinking.

"Don't try this disguise getting him to the hospital,"

Masurik said as he led them through the back. "The Nazis stand inside the door and unwrap every facial bandage coming through."

On the bus ride home, Alex sat with a pencil and paper, juggling numbers. Any other time Jacob would have looked over his shoulder. Now he squeezed his eyes closed and leaned his burning ear against Alex.

The next morning Alex left early. Jacob was surprised he wasn't carrying things to sell. Instead he returned home with a stranger. Jacob quickly hid in the closet.

"Mr. Roslan, you have no idea how much I appreciate your bringing me here to see your apartment," a man with a young voice said.

"I know how difficult housing is these days," Alex replied. "Every day another bomb destroys people's homes."

The man nodded emphatically. "I've been standing in freezing rain for two weeks at the housing authority looking for a place for me and my parents!" the man said. "If only I knew someone who had an apartment to sell—"

Alex made a sweeping gesture with his hand. "Here it is," he said, smiling. The young man looked at the large apartment in disbelief and was about to reply when he saw Mela standing in the doorway with her arms crossed.

"What's going on, Alex?"

"Meet Stepanski, Mela. Stepanski, my wife." To Stepanski he said, "And you won't find many places like this at the price." Stepanski nodded eagerly and walked through the apartment.

"What are you selling, Alex?" Mela persisted, blocking his passage to follow Stepanski. Alex sidestepped her in time to take the money Stepanski removed from his wallet.

"When can we move in?" he asked. Mela wheeled and stared at both men, speechless.

"How about a week?" Alex suggested. Stepanski nodded happily and waved good-bye.

13

Hospital

Mela grabbed the money out of Alex's hands. "What is this?" she demanded.

"I sold the apartment."

Mela sat down on the bed, her face pale. "Stepanski told you how hard it is to find an apartment!" she shouted, unable to hold back her anger. "I don't believe it—how could you!"

Taking her hand, Alex replied, "How could I? Look at your hand. Here's enough money for Genyek's operation. And some left over."

"But we're homeless again," Mela moaned. "Yurek and Marishka haven't gone to school since the last move. I hoped they could start at a new school for next term." She wrung her handkerchief in her hands, her head bent low.

Jacob's Rescue

"Where is he?" Alex asked after a long silence between them. Mela immediately sat up, concerned, and opened the closet door. Jacob lay curled up, holding his ear, asleep. "Up we go, boy," Alex said, gently carrying Jacob into the living room.

"Yurek?" The boy came at once. Handing him a few zlotys, Alex said, "Go down and rent a horse and cart. Bring it to the front of the building and then come help me."

Alex and Mela lay Jacob, still asleep, in the hollowed-out couch. His eyes fluttered open. *Here we go,* he thought wearily. *The mouse in the couch again.* He mumbled, "Where am I going?"

"The hospital," Alex whispered. Mela put a pillow under his head and covered him with a blanket. Then they replaced the cushions. "Are you sure you can trust this Masurik?" Mela asked.

"We have to," Alex replied flatly. When Yurek returned, the two carried the couch down to the street.

"Oh, no, Papa," Yurek whispered. Standing by the cart was a German soldier.

"Come on, son," Alex said loudly. "We have to sell the couch. Let's get on with it."

As Alex and Yurek slid the couch onto the cart, the soldier watched closely. "What's the horse's name?" he asked, stroking the animal's nose.

"Uh," stammered Yurek. "Genyek. He's named after my cousin."

The soldier nodded approvingly and handed the

horse a piece of sugar. "Here, Genyek. Better you than the Jews." He laughed as he walked away. Alex let go of his breath, winked at Yurek, and untethered the horse.

Alex led the horse to the hospital while Yurek kept the sofa steady. At the rear entrance to the building they lifted the heavy piece of furniture onto their shoulders and proceeded down a narrow hallway. "Watch out," Alex hollered. "Coming through."

Halfway down the corridor a nurse stepped in front of the couch. "Where do you think you're going with that thing?" she barked. The sudden stop caused Yurek to lose his grip and almost drop his end of the couch.

Alex answered easily, "To Dr. Masurik's office. He bought it." The nurse looked at the tattered, soiled couch. Alex drew his face near hers and said confidentially, "I can get one for you, too." The nurse grimaced but allowed them to continue to the office.

When Masurik took Jacob from the couch, he noticed blood in Jacob's ear. "We don't have a second to lose," he said, lifting Jacob onto a gurney. "It will be at least two hours."

As the doctor wheeled him into the operating room, Jacob looked up at the gray-bearded face over him, the maze of pipes attached to the high ceiling of the dim hall, and shuddered. "Don't worry, Genyek," Masurik said in a soft voice. "I do this operation all the time—you'll feel fine soon."

The gurney stopped in the middle of a large room. A glaring light shone down on him. A nurse placed a mask over Jacob's face. He inhaled the anesthetic and soon fell asleep.

When he awoke, Alex was holding his hand. "Roslan," the doctor was saying, "Genyek was very brave. I went into the mastoid bone and cleaned out the infection. Lucky you brought him in when you did. Another twenty-four hours and the boy would have died. He can go home tomorrow. Meanwhile," he said with a smile, "I have a new couch."

Alex and Yurek rode home on the horse cart through the once beautiful city of Warsaw. Elegant buildings were reduced to skeletons of steel and concrete. People competed with rats, dogs, and cats for scraps of food.

A German army truck roared into the center of a large space. An SS officer barked into a bullhorn: "All males over the age of sixteen will report to the square immediately! By order of the commandant, Warsaw District." Young men reluctantly emerged from surrounding buildings and stepped into the middle of the square. The voice continued, "German soldiers are being attacked by Polish Partisans. This must stop!"

Alex quickly spun the cart around and headed down a back alley. Machine gun fire behind him confirmed his fear. He looked pointedly at Yurek and said, "Don't even think about joining the Partisans."

Grabbing Yurek by the shoulder, Alex forced him to

look at the square. Bleeding bodies lay crumpled like garbage. "I don't want you to forget what the Germans do to young boys like you."

Scowling, Yurek shook free of his father and stuffed his hands in his pockets, but not before Alex saw them trembling.

14

Runaway

Mela stood in front of a ruin of a building. Several of
the floors had been bombed out, leaving gaping holes
in the brick. Half the windows were boarded up.
"You're not telling me this is our new home," she said
to Alex, her voice wavering. Silence gave her the
dreaded answer. A constant April drizzle made the day
even bleaker.

"Maybe it's nice inside, Mama," Marishka said
doubtfully. They followed Alex into the building, entering a courtyard that once may have been a cheerful
garden of flowers and trees. Now it was a muddy swamp
where nothing grew.

"What's that, Papa?" Yurek asked, pointing at a hole
in the center of the square.

"A well for water."

"A well! Are you saying that we don't have running water in this place?" Mela asked, her voice rising. Alex tried to calm her by leading her toward the apartment. As they descended a dark stairway, the children grew anxious.

The one-room flat was in the basement. Dim light filtered through a few high windows almost opaque with dirt. The walls and ceiling were cracked and peeling. "So, this is where we're going to live." Mela stood in the middle of the room, hands on her hips.

Alex swallowed and nodded. "It just needs a little cleaning and your touch, Mela, to make it home." Marishka and Yurek looked at each other uneasily.

Mela's jaw set hard, and her eyes blazed. "Alex, I can't live like this! In a slum, always running, always afraid we'll be discovered."

Alex moved toward her with his arms out, but she put up a warning hand. "No, I don't want to hear any more. I'm not a hero—" Sarcasm entered her voice. "Not like you. So wonderful. Always helping others!" Mela pointed to her heart. "But what about me? What about our children? When will you help *us*?"

"Mela, calm down. You're upset, you don't know what you're saying," Alex said tentatively.

"Oh, don't I?" she spat out. Her face closed and hardened. "I know exactly what I'm saying. I'm tired." Alex waved his hand dismissively, but Mela continued, "I've had enough. I'm going to the Germans and tell them everything." She turned and ran out the door.

"Papa, stop her!" Yurek and Marishka shouted at once, but Alex was already gone. Yurek threw up his hands in disgust. "Women! They have no guts!"

"Shut up!" Marishka cried. "Do you know anyone else who is doing what Mama and Papa are doing?" Yurek thought for a moment. It was true. He couldn't think of even one family who might be willing to hide a Jew.

"Mama's the one who stays here all day making sure no one finds us," Marishka said. "Even Papa said she has the hardest job."

Even before the war the Roslan family was known for its warmth and generosity. Yurek's and Marishka's friends always wanted to play at their house to sample Mela's delicious cakes. By the steady stream of visitors that came for a day, a week, or a month, the children knew their parents never turned away anyone.

Since Jacob came to stay, however, neither Yurek nor Marishka had been able to bring friends home. They had become adept at the quick lie serving as an excuse whenever anyone suggested coming over.

The door swung open to Alex returning alone, breathing hard and sweating despite the cold. "Don't worry about Mama," he panted, sitting down. "She just needs a little time alone. I know her better than she knows herself," he said soothingly. Had Mela heard this, she would have told him how wrong he was.

He looked at his watch and said to Yurek, "Come on. It's time to pick up Genyek. Mari, you wait here, for Mama." Marishka looked around the barren room and repressed a frightened shiver. If Papa asked, she would do it.

"Move a little faster, Papa," Yurek gasped. "The sofa weighs a ton." Looking ahead, he saw the nurse who had stopped them the day before. "Uh-oh," he said under his breath.

"Where are you going now?" the nurse demanded. Yurek's hands were slippery with sweat.

"Me?" Alex said, as though he had all the time in the world, "Dr. Masurik didn't like the couch. We have to take it back."

The nurse smirked. "No wonder. Get that thing out of here!"

"Yes, ma'am, as quick as we can."

Alex and Yurek hoisted the sofa onto the cart. "Genyek?" Alex whispered loudly. The muffled response from within produced a relieved smile on his face. Jacob was supposedly in the couch when they arrived at the hospital, but of course, Alex hadn't seen him since the operation. Now that he knew he was all right, Alex turned his mind to another problem. Had Mela returned?

Marishka's face told Alex that Mela wasn't back. Sighing with disappointment and worry, he directed Yurek to put the sofa in the middle of the room. Jacob peeped out from under the cushion. He still felt weak from the operation. They all rushed toward him. Suddenly they heard the front door open. All eyes turned from Jacob to Mela standing in the doorway.

"Mela!" Alex exclaimed, "Where have you been?"

"It doesn't matter," she said, patting his face and pushing past him to reach Jacob. She held him for a long time. "Are you feeling better, little mouse?"

He nodded his head wearily, unaware that not only he had been gone from the house. After Mela hugged all the children, she said, "Come, come. Let's not waste time. Let's make this place home."

Alex said, "See, just as I said, everything turns out for the best."

Mela looked up from her broom and shook her head, not bothering to suppress a smile. "Yes, Alex, you're always right." Yurek, Marishka, and Jacob looked at one another, startled, until they caught Mela's wink.

They had been cleaning and unpacking for a few hours when they heard gunshots. Alex and Yurek ran up the stairs, climbing to the roof of the building. "Look, Papa!" Yurek exclaimed. "Fire!"

Alex looked where Yurek was pointing. "My God, that's the ghetto!" Alex shouted. Flames and smoke filled the air as exploding bombs crumpled buildings.

Alex was silent for a moment. "Yurek, remember last week when I was gone almost every night?" The boy nodded intently. "I wasn't bringing food and money into the ghetto as I usually do. This time they wanted only guns and ammunition. The Jews are fighting back."

"Do you think they'll win, Papa?"

"I asked someone in the ghetto why they needed weapons now, and he told me, 'We know the Nazis are about to deport everyone. We have no hope of winning. We will have to fight, and some of us will have to die. The world will not forget April 1943!' They are fighting for their honor, son, not for their lives."

Yurek stared at the burning ghetto. Then something closer to home caught his eye. He squinted and saw moving horses with children on them. "Papa, is that a carousel there?" he asked, pointing just outside the ghetto wall. Alex nodded.

"But how can those people enjoy themselves when—" Yurek couldn't go on. The juxtaposition of amusement and death left him without words.

"Ask Uncle Vladek. No, no, I take that back," he said hastily. "Vladek is all right. He's like most people. Afraid. As long as nothing happens to them, they don't care what happens to anyone else." Marishka was right, Yurek decided. Their family was different from others.

Yurek clenched his fists. He would give anything to have a gun in his hands to kill the first Nazi passing on the street below. Alex looked at him and said, "I'll take you the next time."

"There won't be a next time, Papa. They're killing all the Jews."

"No, not all," Alex said softly. "We have one."

15

David

The destruction of the ghetto shattered the wall Jacob had built to hold back his feelings. He couldn't stop worrying about what was left of his family. Even Uncle Galer hadn't come around since his operation. He hadn't seen Aunt Hannah, his grandmother, or David for two years. He longed to know how they were, but was afraid to ask.

Looking up at the dirt-encrusted window, he heard more than saw feet splashing through puddles. Another gray, rainy day. Not that the weather made any difference to him—it had been a long time since he had seen the outdoors.

From what the Roslans told him, he wasn't missing much—the entire city looked like the ghetto, with sick, starving, and homeless people wandering the streets.

Sighing, Jacob picked up *The Jungle Book* by Rudyard Kipling, eager to leave Poland for the wilds of India.

"Read to me?" Marishka asked, looking up from her mending. Jacob nodded, glad to have his friend along to share the adventure with him. A knock on the door made them both jump. No one had come to their new apartment in the month they had lived there. Jacob stepped into a closet in the bathroom while Marishka looked with worried eyes at her mother.

Mela stood on her toes and peeked through the peephole, relieved to see Galer's familiar little beard. "Come in," she said warmly. Looking at the small boy beside him, Mela smiled warily. "Let me guess. This must be David." The five-year-old grinned, each cheek revealing a deep dimple. Blond ringlets covered his head.

"Where's Jacob?" David piped. Before Mela could answer, Jacob rushed out of the bathroom.

"David!" Jacob shouted, running over to hug his brother. The small boy squealed with pleasure. "You've gotten bigger," Jacob told him. David nodded happily.

The front door swung open. Alex walked into the apartment and pretended surprise at the visitors. "Is someone having a party?"

David looked up and said, "Hi, Alex!" Everyone in the room except Galer blinked surprise.

Mela's eyes narrowed with suspicion as Alex sheepishly began to explain. "Galer thought I should see David; see how he was. So I've been out to the farm a few times. What a mess!" he cried, flinging his arms in the air. Mela waited patiently. "David told me the farmer's ten-year-old daughter kept dragging him into the barn to play doctor. She tried to get him to undress, and he ran out of reasons why he didn't want to."

"As you can see, Galer," Mela said dryly, "we already don't have enough room for the five of us, so what difference can six make?"

Alex clapped his hand on Galer's shoulder and said, "You shouldn't be here at this hour. Let me walk you out." As soon as they were alone, Alex asked, "What happened to the rest of the family?"

Galer burst into tears and said, "Gone. All of them. For me, it's just a matter of time. But—" He broke off, regained his composure, and said, "All that matters is that I helped get my sister's children out. Take care of them, Alex. You are my only hope," Galer turned and left in the foggy rain, unwilling to say good-bye.

Tedek, Little Teddy, as David was called, fit into the family immediately. Everyone, even Yurek, treated him like a pet. "He's so cute!" Marishka squealed, and David beamed, shaking his curls and offering his dimples in reply. In the evening Alex would set David and Marishka on his lap while they combed his hair.

On the other hand, Jacob's delight in having his remaining brother with him quickly wore off. However many times he had dreamed of seeing David again, especially after Sholom's death, Jacob found his presence an intrusion that took attention away from him.

"Even his Polish name is nicer than mine," he fretted. "Genyek. Yah! Yah! Yah! Yah!"

He was so jealous, he could barely speak to or look at David. He not only didn't play with him but never allowed David to participate when he read or played a game with Yurek or Marishka. "You're still a baby, Tedek," Jacob taunted, causing David to cry and scream.

It was July 1944, and the apartment was stifling. Home alone, Jacob stood by the open window taking in the muggy air while David played in the park with Marishka. "It's not fair," Jacob whined to Mela.

Mela shrugged. "What's not fair, Genyek? That the Germans are killing Jews and Poles every day?"

"That his blond hair makes him look Polish and he can go outside!" Jacob shouted.

Overhearing the conversation, Alex put a hand on Jacob's shoulder and interjected, "Genyek, everyone's nerves are tight. Sometimes I think I could slit a throat. I promise, you won't have to stay inside forever."

Jacob was about to protest that he was tired of promises, but he fell silent. Alex and Mela had enough trouble without his complaining. "We'll be back later," Mela said. Alex needed her help in getting a little flour and sugar. "When Marishka comes home, tell her to stay here with David." Jacob responded silently, wanting to disappear into *The Jungle Book*.

David and Marishka returned an hour later, flushed

and sweaty. "Genyek," David panted, running up to Jacob. "Guess what I saw? A dog with three legs!"

"Big deal," Jacob muttered. "Don't bother me. I'm busy."

David hung over his shoulder. "Please show me how to read," he begged. Jacob didn't bother to reply.

"I hate you!" David yelled. Turning to Marishka, he asked, "Can we go back to the park?"

Marishka hesitated, unsure. Before David came, she liked to be home with Jacob. Yurek ignored her, but Jacob insisted that sometimes she be included in their games. When Yurek wasn't around, Jacob needed no coaxing to read or do puzzles with her.

Lately, however, Marishka liked having David as an excuse to go outside. She had begun to feel caged, confined by the house. When she was in the park, she played ball, ran for the pleasure of the free motion. Sometimes she forgot to be afraid.

Although she hungrily searched for old friends, what would she do if she found one? She certainly couldn't walk over and say hello without betraying too much. Her schoolmates had stopped coming to her house the day Genyek came to live with them.

"Hold it," Jacob said, putting his finger in the book to mark his place. "You can't go out. Aunt Mela said she would be gone for two hours. Everyone's supposed to stay here."

"You're just saying that because you can't go out,"

David said. "Marishka, please. I really want to go outside."

Marishka considered this, looking at both boys. "Okay, Tedek. Just for a little while. We have to be back before Mama comes home."

Jacob shook his head. "Don't do it, Dav—Tedek," he warned.

David stuck out his tongue at his brother and left the room, walking hand in hand with Marishka.

16

The Fight

"Let's play hopscotch in front of the building, Tedek," Marishka suggested. With a piece of burned wood, she drew squares on the sidewalk while David looked for a flat stone to use as a marker. Despite the day's grayness, a few flowering plants brightened the street, and people occasionally smiled at the children as they sidestepped the hopscotch court. "It's like there's no war," David said, hopping from square to square.

Marishka was about to agree when her eye caught a German army truck turning the corner. Suddenly the street became deserted. Grabbing David, Marishka yanked him behind a concrete wall next to the building. German soldiers stood up in the truck, firing machine guns at anything that moved. One soldier jumped out of the vehicle and plastered a large poster on a wall. He got back in the truck, and it pulled away, leaving behind a sidewalk littered with dead and wounded. Marishka and David slowly crawled away from their hiding place. Directly in front of them, a woman lay facedown in a puddle of blood. Stepping around her, they saw others lying in the street, some wounded, most dead.

Marishka let out a gasp. A man was dragging the lifeless form of Bobo, the little dog she secretly adopted. She had met the skinny charcoal terrier the first week in the new apartment. Bobo had befriended her instantly. His prominent ribs and lack of a collar told her he was looking for a master. She knew better than to ask her mother if she could keep him. Instead she braided a little collar for him, gave him a name, which he easily learned, and saved a little of her food each day for him. He always met her at the back of the apartment at dusk, wagging his tail.

Bobo had been shot when he had stepped into the street to sniff a body. Marishka ran up to the man hauling Bobo by one leg and asked, "Is that your dog?"

The man snorted. "Are you kidding? This is my dinner." She stood dazed, watching Bobo disappear down the street. Soon it would be her turn to die, too.

David tugged on her arm as she read the poster, which warned all Poles that the Germans would take revenge for Partisan acts. "Come on, Marishka. Let's go upstairs before we get into trouble."

Mela was already home when they walked in. She hugged them both and then scolded, "You could have been killed." Jacob looked up from his book and gave Marishka and David a superior look.

"We're tired of staying in here all the time," Marishka said bitterly. Because her daughter so rarely complained, Mela's face wrinkled with concern. She wanted to probe Marishka's feelings when she noticed Jacob staring at David. The older boy's face was stiff with rage.

"Yeah," David said. "Marishka's right. It's no fun being inside."

Jacob smirked. "Yeah, it's more fun being dead."

"I don't want to be dead!" David cried. Mela squeezed him tighter and put her finger across her lips as a warning to Jacob.

But Jacob was past the stopping point. "No, you just want to be stupid!" he taunted. "I don't even think you're my brother. You're too dumb."

"I am not dumb! I am not stupid!"

"Yes, you are! Dumb and stupid. Stupid and dumb. Dumb and—"

Mela jumped up and, grabbing Jacob by the shoulders, shook him until he became quiet. Never before had she touched him except with affection. "That's enough! Stop this immediately!" she ordered.

Jacob took a deep breath and turned away from David. But David grabbed him and jumped on his back, flailing at his head. "I hope the Gestapo gets you," he screamed, falling off Jacob. He threw himself on the floor and pounded it with his fists.

Jacob cocked his head. He had heard something. "Tedek!" he whispered urgently. "Wait a minute." David stopped long enough to hear a sharp rap at the door.

"You see," Mela said. "You boys have disturbed the neighbors." As she walked to the door, Jacob quickly crawled into the little cupboard in the bathroom. Mela opened the door to a Gestapo agent and two soldiers. Shoving her aside, the agent barked, "Where are the Jews?"

David was frightened but fascinated by the agent. His hair, fingernails, jacket buttons, and shoes gleamed.

"Jews? You want Jews?" Mela shouted, standing as tall as her five feet would allow. "Come and get them! They're all over the place! Can't you see?" she said, making a sweeping gesture with her hand. David sucked his thumb and clung to Mela's skirt while Marishka hid behind them.

Pointing with his thumb, the agent ordered the soldiers, "Go on. Search."

Mela snorted with disgust. "That's right. Search all day and all night. The Jews are inside the walls, the closets. Fifty, a hundred are hiding here."

"Shut up!" the agent snapped. "Your papers—the children's papers." He shouted to be heard over a soldier pounding the walls with his rifle butt. Another soldier slashed his bayonet through the couch. Stuffing flew through the air.

Mela ran to him and tried to rip the rifle out of his hands. She screamed, "You ruin everything! You're destroyers! Get out of here and leave us alone—" The agent pulled her away from the soldier and threw her across the room. Marishka and David, who had been clinging to each other, rushed to her on the floor. Mela sobbed. "Leave us alone."

David watched nervously as one soldier walked over to the bathroom and slammed open cabinets. He flung open one half of the cabinet where Jacob was hiding. Suddenly the agent called, "Enough. There's no one here."

Looking down at David, the agent said, "You have lovely children. Now—their papers!" Mela reached into a drawer and handed him the documents. David's belonged to Alex's nephew Tedek. Staring at David, the agent said, "This one's your nephew?" Mela nodded. The agent smiled and said, "He could almost pass for an Aryan." Mela nodded carefully and watched the three men exit before she spat at the backs of their impeccably tailored uniforms.

17

Uprising

Alex, Mela, and the children huddled around an ancient radio, with Jacob moving the antenna to quiet the static and whistles. Suddenly the broadcaster exuberantly announced: "HELLO, WARSAW SPEAKING! TODAY, AUGUST 1, 1944, THE PEOPLE OF WARSAW ROSE AGAINST THEIR NAZI OPPRESSORS. ALL PEOPLE EVERYWHERE SUPPORT THE COURAGE AND DETERMINATION TO MAKE POLAND FREE ONCE MORE." Jacob and Yurek broke into a cheer until Alex hushed them. The news continued, "THE ARMIES OF THE SOVIET UNION ARE BRACED ON THE OUTSKIRTS OF WARSAW AND WILL BE ENTERING AT ANY MOMENT." The whole family cheered loudly this time.

"Did you see Polish flags flying up and down the

street this morning, Papa?" Yurek asked, jumping up and running around the room like a dog freed of his leash. "I want to see what's happening!"

Alex frowned. "Yurek, I'll tell you when it's safe to go out. Not now. The Polish army is blowing up every German car and building it finds. And don't forget," he added, shaking a finger, "the Germans are more eager than ever to kill any Pole they see. The uprising won't last forever—only when the Russians come in to help us will the streets be safe again."

Yurek had heard enough. As he strode toward the door, Alex shouted, "Yurek, come back!"

Catching up with Yurek at the door leading out of the building, he grabbed the boy's shoulder to stop him. "Where are you going?"

"Papa, we're free! Free! I'm going to get some sugar and horsemeat for us, so we can have a real dinner," Yurek shouted as he ran out of the building. "Don't worry!"

A shot rang out. Alex watched with horror as Yurek crumpled in the middle of the street. Looking up, Alex saw a German sniper duck out of sight from the edge of the roof. He rushed to his son, lifted his limp body, and, as though to give Yurek his strength, hugged him to his chest.

Warm blood soaked Alex's hands and shirt as he carried his dying son into the apartment, all the time screaming, "How dare you! How dare you! Nazi animals!" Mela wept over her son, cursing the Nazis and the war. Marishka stared with unbelieving eyes at her brother's still body. "We have to get him to the doctor," Mela cried.

Yurek opened his eyes, "Mama. Papa. It's all right," he gasped. "I'm sorry I gave you so much trouble." He coughed. Pain coursed through his body. "Take good care of Mari. And Genyek. And Tedek." Yurek had always been full of life, the one to defy orders, and the one who would do anything for a laugh. Now at the end of his life he turned serious.

Alex and Mela took Yurek's body to an empty lot. Alex dug a hole, sweat stinging his eyes as he flung shovelfuls of soil over his shoulder. With Mela's help he delicately laid Yurek into the ground.

Looking down at the newly turned earth that held his son, Alex cursed, wiping away his tears. Mela found a large stone and placed it over the grave. "Yurek," she said. "I'll be back one day to put a real stone here. This is my death," she said, sobbing, as Alex gently pulled her away from Yurek.

Jacob had begged to go with them to bury Yurek, but the Roslans refused—German bombing and shelling took place every day. Jacob knew that, but Yurek was more than a friend and more than a brother. They confided everything to each other. Jacob even carried Yurek's last secret. He hadn't been going out for food, but to join his friends throwing Molotov cocktails at the Germans.

Jacob cried when he first saw Yurek's bleeding body,

but not again. He felt numb, as if nothing could touch him. Fear. No books, games, or puzzles took away this constant fear. "Do you think we'll make it, Mari?" he asked Marishka one day.

She looked steadily at Jacob. "Everyone is dying."

Jacob considered this. Sholom. Aunt Hannah. Now Yurek. He nodded shortly and replied, "It doesn't matter."

Alex walked into the room. "Genyek, it's the only thing that matters." Until Yurek died, Alex never questioned that they would get through the war. But his son's death shook his faith. Now he realized how much they all needed his optimism. "You mustn't give up hope," he said to Jacob and Marishka, lightly putting a hand on each of their shoulders. "There *will* be a better day. I swear it. And—" He paused, winking. "If that isn't true, you can both punch me in the nose. That's a promise." For a brief moment the children weren't afraid.

Every day the family sat by the radio, listening to the underground's battle with the Germans. "Why aren't the Russians here yet?" everyone asked. Shellings and bombings shook the streets as the Nazis crumpled Warsaw with their weapons. No one went out without risking his life. Even Alex stayed in the apartment during the day.

When the bombs fell next door, Alex waited until dark and then quickly moved the family to a shelter. David clung to Mela as they entered the large, cold room heavy with the smell of unwashed people. Jacob had never seen so many Poles. He edged near Alex, who grabbed his hand and squeezed.

The family had been in the shelter for a month when they were awakened in the middle of the night by the sound of bombs exploding everywhere. Alex fumbled in the dark for the radio. As soon as it came on, everyone in the basement shelter crowded around to hear, "HELLO, WARSAW SPEAKING! THIS CITY OF ONE MILLION PEOPLE IS BEING WIPED OUT. WE HAVE GIVEN MORE THAN WE COULD. WE ARE TODAY THE CONSCIENCE OF THE WORLD. WE WERE CALLED THE 'INSPIRATION OF THE FIGHTING NATIONS AND THE INSPIRATION OF THE WORLD.' WE, AS A NATION, HAVE A RIGHT TO LIVE! WE DEMAND THAT RIGHT!" Static signaled the end of the broadcast.

The room filled with the sounds of cries, sighs, people blowing their noses, and angry shouts. Alex sat quietly after he shut off the radio, his hand over his mouth, staring at the floor. David, sitting on Jacob's lap, wanted to talk, but Jacob put his hand over his brother's mouth, waiting.

Alex felt the family's eyes on him. "We have to get out of Warsaw," he whispered. "The Germans will kill every Pole they find—they want revenge for the uprising."

Mela suggested, "Alex, let's go to Vladek's little village. He told me he doesn't even know there's a war."

Alex shook his head and allowed himself a chuckle. "I never thought I'd have any use for your brother."

Mela shook a finger at him, but she smiled.

"Children," Alex said, standing up. "We leave tonight. Take only what you absolutely have to, because we'll be walking."

18

Escape

"Sh!" Alex whispered to the children shivering outside
the shelter. Across the road a large field of yellow wheat
rose tall against the gloomy sky. The sun had set a half
hour before, and the chill of the fall day penetrated
their threadbare clothes. "One by one we will go and
hide in the wheat until it's completely dark. Genyek,
you go first," he instructed, pointing to the wheat field.

Alex's quiet, calm voice steadied Jacob as he lifted
his knapsack and slipped across the road to disappear
into the field. He thrashed through the tall stalks until
he was completely protected from view. He saw nothing
but wheat in all directions. It began to rain. When
Marishka found him, Jacob was shaking from cold and
fear. She couldn't tell if his face was wet from rain or
tears.

When everyone reached the hiding place, they waited in silence, motionless and alert, listening while the Germans marched thousands of Poles out of Warsaw onto trains heading for concentration camps.

Bombs exploded without warning, causing everyone to jump. Alex looked up and whispered, "We're lucky. It's a new moon, a dark night. Let's cross the highway and look for a farm."

Alex crouched low, keeping his eyes sharp for German soldiers. After a guard passed by, Alex whistled low for the family to cross the road, following closely behind him. Along the highway other small bands of people also fled the city.

As the rain pelted them, David wailed, "Help!" Jacob looked behind him and found David fallen and stuck in the mud. Stepping back, Jacob pulled him up. They were in the middle of a field.

"Here," he said, wrapping an arm around his brother. "Lean against me." David's muddy face was streaked with tears.

Alex came up alongside the boys. "Make believe you're rabbits," he said, "lightly bouncing across the field." He imitated a rabbit hop. David giggled at Alex's comic jumps.

Jacob groaned as he trudged along with aching legs. "I feel more like a hippopotamus caught in quicksand." Alex patted him on the head and moved on to help Mela and Marishka, whose skirts made walking almost impossible. Alex insisted that the family plod on, stopping only to relieve themselves or have a morsel to eat and drink.

Hours passed. "Papa, look!" Marishka pointed in the darkness. An outline of a roof emerged through the rain. Moving as quickly as the mud allowed, Alex went back and put David on his shoulders. By the time they reached the building, an old barn, David was fast asleep.

Jacob opened the door and jumped back from the humming din. Refugees packed the barn. Alex pushed forward and found a tiny space for the five of them. Mela opened a sack and took out dry clothes for everyone. "Here. Get into these," she ordered. "Nobody is allowed to get sick."

As they undressed, the children looked shyly around the barn, but no one looked at them. Everyone was too tired and scared to pay attention to anything except themselves. The exhausting hike, the comfort of dry clothes, and the rhythmic patter of rain tapping the roof soon relaxed the family into a dreamless, deep sleep.

At daybreak Mela woke the children. "Take a little bread and jam," she murmured as she handed them the food. When they finished eating, they gathered their things and continued on their journey. The morning was freezing but brilliantly clear.

Jacob looked behind, to the east. Warsaw was in flames. He allowed his imagination to play a game that had begun when he entered the ghetto three years before. *Maybe I'll go back one day, and everything and everyone will still be there, waiting for me,* he told himself. His parents, grandparents, aunts and uncles, and servants would all be in the house. He could hear their voices and smell a pot roast cooking. Outside, Stasek would be slowly caressing the blue Buick's already lustrous finish.

"How much farther to Vladek's?" David asked.

"Kaminsk is probably another twelve miles," Alex answered. David rolled his eyes but said nothing.

They walked all day, seeing no one but an occasional farmer working in the fields. They rested only once, in a cow pasture, where Alex stopped long enough to get some milk for them. By dusk David began to cry, and Alex carried him on his back.

"I see a little building ahead, Alex," Mela said. "I think we should sleep in it tonight. The children can't go farther." Alex nodded halfheartedly; being on the run was dangerous, and he wanted to reach Kaminsk that night.

"Uncle Alex," Jacob called, "that building is a train station." He squinted at the letters on the roof. "Ka—m—insk!" he shouted. "We're here!"

"Put me down," David said sleepily to Alex. "I can run faster than anyone."

"All right, Tedek," Alex said. "Lead the way." David ran ahead, with Jacob and Marishka easily gaining on and overtaking him.

Jacob and Marishka looked at the three buildings beside the train depot and then at each other. "This is Kaminsk?" Jacob asked.

Marishka shrugged, doubtful. "Let's wait for my father."

When the Roslans reached them moments later, Marishka asked, "Is this it?" She swept her arms at the one street with a few houses tucked behind it. Alex and Mela nodded, then smiled at each other. They had grown up in a village like this one, but their children knew only Warsaw. Mela walked up to one of the houses and knocked on the door.

A rumpled Vladek stood in the door, blinking at his visitors before he shouted, "Mela! Alex! I don't believe it!"

"Someone answered your sister's prayers," Alex said dryly.

"Come in, all of you," Vladek said. "Have a little tea to warm you up." In the house a fire of dry branches crackled cheerfully, and one by one they sat around it. After Vladek poured tea, he said, "The war doesn't exist here. No Germans. No one bothers you."

Mela burst into tears. "Vladek, we thought we'd never make it."

"Speak for yourself, Mela," Alex objected.

Vladek leaned toward Alex and Mela, and said softly, "But you must understand. No one here wants trouble." Alex and Mela looked at him warily. Vladek went on,

"What I mean is, the Jews—how long have you had them? Three years? Isn't that enough?"

Jacob, pretending not to hear, poked the fire expertly, his jaw clenched. He hated Vladek, even if he was Mela's brother. Then he remembered what Alex had told him. Most people are like Vladek. The thought didn't make him feel better.

"That's not your business," Mela snapped. "We'll leave," she said, getting up.

"Calm down, sister," Vladek said hastily, catching her hand. "Just be careful."

The following week Alex and Jacob helped Sawicki, the local baker, repair an old hearth. Jacob liked to mix the mortar and watch Alex meticulously lay bricks in the oven. "Nice job, Roslan," the baker said at the end of the day. "What do I owe you?"

Without hesitating, Alex answered, "A loaf of bread."

Jacob thought, *If stomachs could smile, mine would be grinning a kilometer wide.*

"Good, because I don't have any money," said the baker, handing him two long loaves of coarse black bread.

Alex smiled. "Why should you be different from anyone else?"

Sawicki drew close to Alex. "Roslan, it will soon be over. The Russians are just across the river."

"Sure." Alex snorted. "I've been hearing that for a long time. Look, it's been months. The uprising started last August. Remember? Now it's already 1945. What are the Russians waiting for? The Germans to kill us first?"

Sawicki was about to protest when Alex smiled. "If it makes you feel better to believe, believe. Call me again if you need help," he said, exiting with Jacob. They were walking toward the house when they saw Vladek running toward them.

"Alex, we're in trouble," he said breathlessly. "Some people, neighbors, are accusing you of being Jewish." Jacob turned white.

Thrusting the bread in the boy's arms, Alex hissed, "Genyek, go upstairs! I'll be back soon." Turning to Vladek, he said, "Take me to your doctor!"

A startled Vladek led Alex to a small building a block away. Marching past a room of waiting patients and a shocked nurse, Alex barged into the doctor's office. "I want a certificate that proves I'm not a Jew!"

Since only Jews were circumcised, a quick examination convinced the doctor that Alex wasn't Jewish. He hastily filled out a certificate. As Vladek began to apologize for his brother-in-law's rudeness, Alex grabbed his elbow and led him out the door.

"Here." Alex thrust the paper at Vladek. "Show this to your neighbors. Tell them next time they may be the accused!"

Vladek shook his head in amazement. *Roslan may be a fool,* he thought, *but he has guts.*

19

Freedom

The certificate became a magic wand. Overnight the town accepted the Roslan family without question— Vladek graciously accepted compliments about them.

They still suffered, however. January brought an exceptionally harsh winter, freezing everything, even rain. The family slept together to keep from being frozen themselves. David slept in the middle and was always warm. Jacob slept poorly, awakening throughout the night with chattering teeth.

One night he picked up his head and saw Marishka staring into space. "Want to play 'words'?" he mouthed soundlessly. She smiled eagerly, relieved to be distracted from not being able to fall asleep.

On two scraps of paper Jacob wrote down the longest word he could think of, handing one to Marishka. They quickly raced against each other to create the most words from the letters of the original word.

Jacob had taught Marishka this game three years before, when they were both eight. It was only one of the things they enjoyed doing together. The war had thrown them tightly together and had forced them to amuse each other. Yet it was more than circumstances that made them close. From the moment they met, they felt a special understanding between them. Even in Kaminsk, where they were free to go outside and the local children were eager to play with them because they were from the big city, they still kept to themselves.

When Yurek had been alive, sometimes Jacob had felt torn between Marishka and her brother. Since his death, the two had become best friends, who could tell each other anything. Once Jacob had boldly told Marishka, "I hope we'll always be together. When we grow up, I'll marry you!"

Jacob and Marishka didn't disturb the sleeping figures around them while they labored to outwit each other. Suddenly the window rattled. The children locked frightened eyes, waiting. It happened again. Creeping to the window, they looked out at the snow-covered ground sparkling beneath the moon and spied a dark shape scooping up pebbles to throw against the window.

Jacob waved down at the figure, who looked up. "Sawicki!" he exclaimed, and opened the window to a blast of frigid air.

"Get your father," the man whispered hoarsely.

Marishka shook Alex awake. "Sawicki's outside. He wants to talk to you."

Alex rubbed the sleep from his eyes, pulled on his coat, and walked outside. Jacob, wrapped in a blanket, followed him.

Sawicki exclaimed, "Roslan, my father is a colonel with the Partisans."

"So?" Alex yawned, annoyed to be awakened for what seemed to be useless information.

"So don't go to sleep tonight! My father says at two in the morning, the Russians will be here."

Alex grew angry. "For this you woke me up? We've already had this conversation, Sawicki. Always the Russians. And they never come." He took Jacob by the hand and walked inside.

"Won't they ever come?" Jacob asked.

Alex shrugged. "When it happens, then we'll celebrate." Despite Alex's pessimism, no one went back to sleep. In the darkness Alex frequently squinted at his watch. "Well, it's five to two," he announced. "I don't hear anything." Jacob and Marishka held up crossed fingers.

Suddenly a great explosion erupted over the countryside. The land lit up as if a million flashbulbs exploded. The bed trembled and the house shook. Like a steel wall, the Soviet army was advancing against the whole of Poland.

From the window the Roslans and the children

watched German soldiers running through the village, dropping their weapons and anything else too heavy to carry in their frantic retreat. "Look!" Jacob screamed. "Russian tanks!"

David grabbed Jacob and pulled him onto the bed. "We're free! We're free!" they yelled, jumping up and down until the bed broke beneath their weight. They collapsed with giggles when the first Russian soldier came to the door.

Jacob rushed to open it. In front of him stood one of the largest human beings he had ever seen. The soldier, wrapped in a thick, padded jacket, had a heavy, black, curly beard and fierce eyes. Startled, Jacob found himself in the man's arms, being swung around and around. The soldier held him out at arm's length and stared at him.

"You're Jewish," he stated matter-of-factly.

Jacob froze. Slowly he nodded his head.

The soldier broke out in a broad grin. "Me, too!"

20

My Sons

The war ended in May 1945. Alex decided to take the family to Berlin. "Berlin? Why Berlin?" Vladek asked, mystified why anyone would want to live anywhere but in Kaminsk.

Mela answered, "Because that's where Jewish agencies are looking for relatives of Jewish families. If the boys have any family left, we'll find them."

"Then you'll finally be finished with these kids?"

Mela looked ready to slap her brother. "No, Vladek, these are our children, just like Marishka and—" she paused, dropping her voice, "Yurek. As long as they want, they will stay with us. But maybe they have a cousin alive somewhere."

Although the war was over, peace was only a dream for the millions of refugees pouring into Berlin. The city, divided into American, British, French, and Russian zones, was overcrowded with conquering armies and survivors of the war.

Entering the British section first, the Roslans went to the authorities to fill out the necessary forms for settling in the city. The British officer in charge looked at Alex and Mela incredulously. "You're saying that these two are not really your children? They're Jews that you hid during the war?" Marishka nodded proudly until she looked at the man's face.

"This puts a different stamp on things," he replied. "There is no way you can keep these children. We'll have to find proper homes for them."

Alex leaned across the desk and stared deeply into the officer's eyes. "For almost four years we've had the boys. They are like our own. No—they *are* our sons! I will not have you take them away."

The officer asked, "You are not Jewish, are you?"

"What does it matter?" Alex responded, his voice rising.

"Makes all the difference in the world. Seems to me you'd be more interested in your own kind."

Jacob winced. Marishka squeezed his elbow. "They are our own kind," Mela said quietly.

"Well, no matter," the officer said briskly. "All of them, the girl, too, must go to special housing to be examined and strengthened with proper food. Every child coming to Berlin must go through this process."

Alex grimaced. "You like that word, 'proper.' No

thanks. We don't need 'proper' help. The children are healthy. I promised we would survive, and that's what we did," he finished, his voice breaking.

But the officer was not moved and insisted that regulations had to be followed. They could visit the children on weekends. "At least we'll be together," David whispered to Jacob. But Jacob was looking at Marishka. She would be all by herself in the girls' dormitory.

Several weeks later, on a Sunday, the children were visiting the Roslans when a representative of the Jewish Agency called on them. She pulled documents out of her briefcase and placed them on a table. "I have good news for you," she stated. They all leaned forward expectantly. Was the family going to be allowed to live together finally?

"I think we've found the boys' father." The woman's words hung in the air as everyone tried to understand.

In his mind Jacob had buried his father along with the rest of his family years ago. "I thought he was dead," he said.

"No. He escaped before the Germans came in and apparently made his way down to Turkey and into Palestine. He's been living there ever since," the representative explained.

Alex shook his head with disbelief. "Does he know about the children?"

By now the woman knew her news was not a cause for celebration. She said quietly, "A wire was sent. He asked that they join him as soon as possible."

"No!" Jacob shouted. "It's not true! *He's* my father," grabbing Alex's arm. "You always have been," he said to Alex.

"I don't want to leave you!" David cried, unsure of what was happening.

"Mama," Marishka asked, "can't we all go to Palestine?"

Mela smiled, looking at Alex. "Why not?"

"I'll tell the British we want to take you there ourselves," Alex asserted. "After all, who knows you better than we do?"

Jacob nodded vigorously, sure that Alex would find a way. Besides, who took children from their family? Anyway, if their father *was* alive, he didn't deserve to have his sons back, because he had deserted them. Jacob didn't even want to know a man like that.

Alex pounded his fist on the counter, causing the clerk to step back. "Don't tell me I can't go! These are my children, and I have a right to take them to Palestine."

Others in the office stared at Alex. The clerk attempted a weak smile. "Sir, there are quotas on how many people can go into the country. You're lucky they're letting the boys in. But you're not even Jewish. Why in the world would you want to go to Palestine?"

"Because if that's where Genyek and Tedek are living, then I belong there, too!"

"I'm sorry," she said, stamping Jacob and David's entry visas, "there's nothing more I can do." She shoved the documents toward Alex, who snatched them up and strode out of the office.

Back home Alex told the boys what happened. Shaking his head, he murmured, "In the beginning I never thought you would be with us for more than a month or two. Now I can't remember a time without you."

As the Roslans packed up the boys' belongings, including the suits Alex had made especially for the boys to wear when they got off the boat to meet their father, Alex explained their journey.

"The train will take you to a place called Lisbon, Portugal. Someone from the Jewish Agency will meet you and put you on a boat that's going to Cyprus. Then you'll take another boat to Palestine," he said, blowing his nose.

"I'll run away," David announced.

Mela shook her head. "I'll be very angry with you. You have a father. He misses you very much."

"If he missed us so much, why did he leave?" Jacob challenged angrily. "We could have been killed. He didn't do anything to protect us. Only you did!"

"He didn't know, Genyek. No one had any idea of what monsters the Nazis would be."

The following day they all went to the railroad station, where they were met by a woman from the Jewish Agency. Part of Jacob longed to jump on the train immediately to end the torture of the farewell. Yet he couldn't bring himself to leave the Roslans. When the woman told them to board the train, Jacob became stone. He kissed Alex and Mela quickly and stepped up on the train. But when Marishka came over to him and asked, "Who will help me with my math?" Jacob swallowed and turned away, not wanting her to see his tears.

"One of these days we'll all be together," he promised her. He looked down. "Remember, I'm going to marry you," he whispered.

She nodded. "I'll never forget."

The boys climbed on board, all the time waving to the Roslans. Alex, Mela, and Marishka stood at the station a long time after the train disappeared from view.

21

Reunion

Jacob paused in the story. "Have I answered all your questions, Marissa?" he asked gently. Her father's words brought her back to the present.

Marissa didn't answer at once. Almost everything her father told her seemed to fit. His slight Polish accent, how he survived the war, how he ended up in Israel, who the Roslans were. But her father's story opened new questions.

"What happened to Marishka?" she asked hesitantly, afraid of the answer. Obviously her father had not married Marishka. She could barely look at her father.

To her relief Jacob's serious face brightened into a smile.

Before he could answer her questions, David broke in and asked Jacob, "May I tell this part?" He and his brother rarely talked about the war years. Jacob always wanted to put the time "past them," as he said.

For David those years were like a dream he couldn't quite remember. He possessed little recollection of his childhood. Although he wasn't an orphan, he grew up feeling he missed some important information about who he was.

David began, "Please, let me tell the rest of the story, because this is the only part I know." Looking at the Roslans, he said, "I'll never forget leaving you at the train station." Alex's chin trembled, and Mela dabbed her eyes.

"After we went to Palestine," David told Marissa, "Alex, Mela, and Marishka went to America, to New York."

"Did you call one another?"

David and Jacob chuckled. "In those days Israel had maybe six telephones," David answered.

Alex said, "No, we wrote. I wrote the boys every week. But I never got an answer."

"It's true," Jacob said reluctantly. "Our father didn't give us the letters. And all the cards we sent to Alex and Mela—and the letters I sent to Marishka—didn't reach them, because our father never mailed them."

"Why?" cried Marissa at her grandfather.

Her grandfather hunched forward in his chair. "There are things people do that they are ashamed of," he said in a wavering voice just above a whisper. "I didn't know the truth of what happened in those days.

When I heard about the Roslans, I was all mixed up. I was happy they had saved my sons, but Alex had taken my place! Mela had become their mother! I didn't think they could love the Roslans and love me. I only wanted my sons back."

The room fell silent after Mr. Gutgeld's words. He kept his eyes down, far from anyone else. Alex cleared his throat. "But after sixteen years the boys found us!" he exclaimed. "They were both studying in California, and they asked enough people. First we saw David, then Jacob."

"But this is the first time we have all been together," David said, "since the war. That's why this seder is different from others, the most special of all." He swallowed, for a moment unable to speak. "Your father and I had the idea to bring Alex and Mela to Israel for Passover. Marishka couldn't come because she couldn't leave her children."

Marissa grinned with relief. Marishka was alive.

"We spoke with her last week," Jacob added. "She hopes to come with her family this summer."

"Dad," Marissa blurted, "am I named for her?"

Jacob smiled, his eyes soft. "Well, little one, your mother and I liked the name. And . . . I am glad I still have a Mari in my life." Although Marissa had always known her name was unusual, she liked the sound of it. Now she liked it even more.

David said, "Your father and I arranged for the Israeli government to give Alex and Mela the Righteous

Among the Nations award, the medal Israel gives only to non-Jews who risked their lives to save Jews during the Holocaust."

Marissa looked at Alex and Mela with new respect. She had studied the Holocaust in school and had learned about these brave, few people. But she hadn't known any of them still lived. Now she was sitting next to two of them. "I wouldn't be here if it weren't for you," she said, suddenly shy.

Alex shook his head. "Don't think about that. Would you like to see the medal?"

Marissa nodded eagerly. From his pocket Alex withdrew what looked like a large bronze coin. He handed it to Marissa, who squinted at the writing around the edges. "That's the part I like best," Alex said.

Marissa slowly read, "Whoever saves a single life is as one who has saved the entire world." She looked at Alex and Mela, and then at her father and uncle. "One more question," she said. "Is there a special medal if you save two lives?"

Afterword

If the story you just read had been imagined, you would probably dismiss it as too farfetched. You might think no one is that good or that bad. But the Roslan family and the Gutgeld brothers are real people, and this book is about what happened to them. Of course, many years have passed and each person remembers things differently, so the story told here cannot be an exact recreation of events.

We know this—they all lived through the darkest period of modern history. From 1939 to 1945 Adolf Hitler and his followers tried to make Germany the ruling country of the world. They crushed and destroyed any individual or nation that attempted to stop them. With armed soldiers and tanks, the Nazis invaded nearly every country in Europe. They used brutal force to make nations accept Germany's rule.

In addition to his plan to be master of the world, Hitler burned with another passion. He wanted to eliminate Jews from the human race. If just one person wished this, it would only have been a mad and vicious idea. But Hitler was a master at spreading hatred and mistrust. He convinced the Germans that Jews were to blame for virtually every social problem. Many Germans were out of work and poor. Hitler gave them someone to blame for their suffering.

He took his message of hate to Holland, Belgium, France, Italy, Yugoslavia, Hungary, Czechoslovakia, Rumania, Russia, and Poland. In every country some of the people believed him. By the war's end the Nazis, with help from each country in rounding up and deporting Jews, killed six million Jews as well as seven million others that Hitler declared inferior. The death camps were mostly in Eastern Europe. The Nazis wanted countries such as Denmark, Holland, and France to think the Germans were civilized human beings, not barbaric murderers. But since they regarded Poles and the other Slavs as contemptible, they put the ovens for burning bodies in their countries.

Most Europeans didn't believe, ignored, or turned away from the suffering of Jews. They didn't want to know about starvation, firing squads, or gas chambers.

But a few people would not look away. They rescued most of the Jews who survived the war. Alex and Mela

Roslan were two of those rescuers. They risked their lives to save three Jewish children, Jacob, Sholom, and David Gutgeld from the Warsaw ghetto in 1941. They hid the children until January 1945, when Germany retreated from Poland in defeat.

After the war the Roslan family never talked about what they had done. Until they were all given a medal in 1981 at Yad Vashem, the Holocaust Memorial in Israel, Alex and Mela had never received any honor or reward for their moral courage. Although they are proud of the medal, they don't need it. Their greatest reward has always been the love of the children they saved, who consider them to be their parents.

But the brothers have always wanted everyone to know that they are alive because of the Roslans. This is not only because they are grateful but because they believe it's important for all of us to remember that even in the worst of times, goodness still exists.

None of us knows whether we possess the capacity for heroism. It often takes crisis to reveal this part of ourselves. Perhaps only a few people can be as selfless and courageous as the Roslans, but everyone can pay attention to another's suffering and try to help.

Jacob, Alex, and David soon after they arrived in Berlin.
(Courtesy of Alex and Mela Roslan)

Alex and Mela
Roslan today,
in their backyard
in Clearwater,
Florida.
*(Copyright © 1992
by Gay Block)*

Jacob today, with his wife, Geulah. *(Courtesy of Michael Halperin)*

David at a tribute
to the Roslans at
the Simon
Wiesenthal
Center in
Los Angeles.
*(Copyright © 1992 by
Long Photography,
Inc.)*